$\mathcal{O}$utside
THE LAW

Also by Robert J. Conley in Large Print:

Border Line
The Gunfighter
The Long Trail North
Strange Company
To Make a Killing
Wilder & Wilder
A Cold Hard Trail
Fugitive's Trail

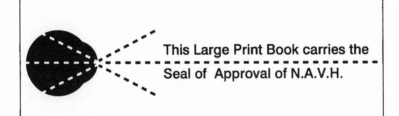

This Large Print Book carries the
Seal of Approval of N.A.V.H.

Outside
THE LAW

Robert J.
CONLEY

WHEELER
PUBLISHING

Published in 2004 by arrangement with
Cherry Weiner Literary Agency.

Wheeler Large Print Western.

The text of this Large Print edition is unabridged.
Other aspects of the book may vary from the original edition.

Set in 16 pt. Plantin.

Printed in the United States on permanent paper.

Library of Congress Cataloging-in-Publication Data

Conley, Robert J.
    Outside the law / Robert J. Conley.
       p. cm.
    ISBN 1-58724-623-6 (lg. print : sc : alk. paper)
    1. Classicists — Crimes against — Fiction.   2. Teachers — Crimes against — Fiction.   3. Tahlequah (Okla.) — Fiction.   4. Cherokee women — Fiction.   5. Sheriffs — Fiction.   6. Large type books.   I. Title.
    PS3553.O494O93 2004
    813'.54—dc22   2004041937

Outside
THE LAW

National Association for Visually Handicapped
----------------------- *serving the partially seeing*

As the Founder/CEO of NAVH, the only national health agency solely devoted to those who, although not totally blind, have an eye disease which could lead to serious visual impairment, I am pleased to recognize Thorndike Press* as one of the leading publishers in the large print field.

Founded in 1954 in San Francisco to prepare large print textbooks for partially seeing children, NAVH became the pioneer and standard setting agency in the preparation of large type.

Today, those publishers who meet our standards carry the prestigious "Seal of Approval" indicating high quality large print. We are delighted that Thorndike Press is one of the publishers whose titles meet these standards. We are also pleased to recognize the significant contribution Thorndike Press is making in this important and growing field.

Lorraine H. Marchi, L.H.D.
Founder/CEO
NAVH

* Thorndike Press encompasses the following imprints: Thorndike, Wheeler, Walker and Large Pr int Press.

—1—

Tahlequah, Cherokee Nation, 1873

The Cherokee National Council had adjourned the day before, and many of the people who had gathered for that occasion in Tahlequah, the capital city, had already left town. But there were some still hanging around. Some of the rowdies were not yet through having a good time, and others, good citizens, were not done visiting friends or relatives in the vicinity.

Sheriff Go-Ahead Rider, formerly sheriff of Tahlequah District, and recently appointed high sheriff of the Cherokee Nation, had dismissed all of the special deputies he had hired specifically for the busy time of the council meeting. Special Deputy Delbert Swim, who had spent the night working in the jail, had been the last to be released from duty. Between himself and George Tanner, his regular full-time deputy, things were manageable from here, Rider thought.

It was an early December morning, and a damp chill was in the air. The cells in the Cherokee National Prison were full of drunks and rowdies, but most of them were quiet after having spent some time in jail. Some were pretty badly hungover, or "sick," as they preferred to say. Rider had gone to his office in the National Prison early, intending to empty out the cells as much as possible.

He had no one incarcerated there who seemed to constitute a real threat to the public peace. Drunk, they had been a public nuisance; in jail, they were a nuisance only for Rider, and an unnecessary expense for the Nation. Most of them would be turned out with a warning to behave themselves. A few would be given court dates and released. Rider was anxious to get rid of them and have a little peace and quiet around the place again.

He stoked up the fire in the wood burner to get a little more heat in the office and so he could put some coffee on to boil, but before he could get water for the pot, George Tanner walked in.

"Good morning, Rider," said George, taking off his hat and hanging it on a wall peg beside the door. "It's getting colder out there."

"Morning, George," said Rider. "You're out and around early. I figured with the council meeting over, you'd sleep in this morning. Stay warm in bed with that pretty wife of yours."

"Ha," said George. "The baby won't let that happen."

"How is my little namesake?"

"Oh, he's just fine," said George, reaching for the coffeepot. "Here. Let me do that."

Rider handed the pot to George and went

8

to his big desk. He sat down and opened a drawer, in which he searched for some papers. Finding the right forms, he pulled them out, shut the drawer, and tossed the forms on top of the desk.

This was the part of his job that he did not care for — filling out forms, making reports: paperwork. He didn't mind rounding up law-breakers, investigating complaints, breaking up fights, even dealing with occasional dangerous criminals, but he could sure have done without all the paperwork.

George had put the pot of water on top of the stove and was reaching for the bag of coffee when they heard the shot. He looked quickly at Rider, who had already gotten to his feet.

"Let's go, George," said Rider, picking up the two Colts from his desktop and thrusting them into his waistband as he stood. George was the first one outside, but Rider was close behind, pulling his hat down onto his head. Since the office had not yet warmed up, both men were still wearing their coats. It was a good thing — the air was cold outside. They stopped for a moment and stood side by side at the foot of the steps that led up to the front porch of the two-story stone building that was the Cherokee National Prison, as the jail was officially called.

"Where do you think it came from?" asked George.

"I couldn't tell," said Rider.

They looked around, but neither man saw anything out of the ordinary. Then another shot sounded, and Rider started to run toward Muskogee Avenue, the main street of Tahlequah, a block west of where the prison stood.

"The livery stable," he shouted. "Come on."

As he ran he pulled a big Colt out of the waistband of his trousers. Close behind him, George drew his Starr revolver out of its holster. When he had first gone to work for Rider, George had tried to carry the revolver in his pants the way Rider did his, but he had found it much too uncomfortable. The belt and holster worked a whole lot better for him.

Two more shots were fired from the vicinity of the livery stable as they ran toward it, and Rider, waving at George to follow him, ducked behind a small shack just across the street from their destination. From this position he could see the far southwest corner of the building, and there he saw the man with the gun. He appeared to be hiding and shooting around the corner. His opponent must have been at the other corner — the northwest — at the rear of the stable.

"I see him, George," said Rider. "Take a look."

George peeked around the corner of the shack.

10

"Yeah," he said. "I see him. Looks like he's in a gunfight with someone."

"Looks that way, don't it," said Rider. "Well, we don't want to rush them from here — we might get ourselves shot. Why don't you just amble on down the street thataway and sneak up on the back side of the other fellow. I'll try to do the same with this one here."

"Okay," said George, and he started to walk north.

"George," said Rider. "Be careful."

"Yes sir."

Rider let George get well away from him before he made his own move. As long as he was quiet, he figured, he shouldn't have any trouble. The shooter's full attention seemed to be well occupied with his opponent. Rider thought that he could probably just walk casually up behind the man and get the drop on him. He moved in a direct line, calculated to allow him to do just that.

About halfway across, he recognized the man. It was Orren Harkey. Rider kept walking. He wanted to get as close as possible before Harkey realized that anyone was behind him. A few paces away, Rider stopped and leveled his Colt at Harkey.

"Orren," he said. Harkey turned quickly, pressing his back against the side wall of the stable. His own revolver, in his right hand, was about halfway up to firing position.

"Don't raise that shooter. I'd hate to have to put a hole in you."

"Rider," said Harkey. "Son of a bitch is trying to kill me."

"Put the gun down, Orren," said Rider.

"Well, what about him?" said Harkey.

"I said put it down, and I ain't going to say it again."

Harkey turned his head as if to look for his enemy, then looked back toward Rider, but his eyes focused on the barrel of the big Colt, which was aimed generally at his midsection. He was well acquainted with the reputation of Go-Ahead Rider — Captain Go-Ahead Rider of Civil War fame. He opened his fingers and let his revolver drop to the dirt.

"Turn around and press your face against the wall," said Rider. Harkey turned, and Rider walked over and picked up the weapon, tucking it in his pants. Then, his right hand on Harkey's back, pushing him into the wall, and his Colt in his left hand, he eased himself around the corner to take a peek. The man at the other corner raised a gun, and Rider ducked behind the wall just as a shot was fired.

"I told you, Rider," said Harkey. "He's crazy."

"Who is it, Orren?" asked Rider.

"Hell, it's old Bob Avery, that's who it is. He seen me talking to Suzy Potter and took after me. Just talking to her. That's all."

"Avery," called out Rider. "You hear me?"

"Who the hell are you?" screamed Avery.

"I'm the sheriff. Toss out your gun and step forward with your hands high."

"You go to hell," said Avery. "You can't touch me. I'm a white man."

Just then George Tanner stepped up behind Avery, raised his Starr up high, and brought the barrel crashing down on top of Avery's head. Avery dropped to the ground like a sack of flour. George leaned over to pick up the gun.

"It's okay, Rider," he shouted. "I got him."

Rider, pushing Harkey ahead of him, walked around the building to join George. He looked down at the seemingly lifeless Avery.

"You didn't kill him, did you?" he asked.

"I just thumped him on the head," said George.

"Is he right about what he said?" asked Harkey. "You can't do nothing to him 'cause he's a white man?"

"Orren," said Rider, letting out a long breath that looked like a puff of smoke in the cold air, "a little knowledge of the law is sometimes a dangerous thing."

Later that morning, George Tanner sat in a café on Muskogee Avenue across the table from Christopher Lang. It was a Saturday, and Lang, a teacher of classics at the Cherokee Male Seminary, did not have to be at work. He had stopped by the jail to see if George had time for coffee and a short visit. Rider had told his deputy to go ahead.

"Things seem to be pretty quiet around here — finally," Rider had said.

He knew that George, who had a degree in the classics himself, had developed a real friendship with the new teacher. Up until Lang's arrival in Tahlequah just four months before, the only person George could discuss his major interest with was his wife, Lee, so Rider didn't begrudge George a little time off on a quiet day for a visit with Lang.

"I heard gunshots earlier this morning," said Lang. "Is everything all right?"

"Yeah," said George. "It is now. We had a couple of fellows trying to kill each other, but we've got them locked up."

"In separate cells, I hope," said Lang.

George chuckled.

"Naturally," he said.

"What was the fight all about?" asked Lang.

"A woman."

"Were they Indians?"

"One of them is a Cherokee citizen," said George, "but he's really more white than Indian. The other man is white."

"You know, George," said Lang, "this Cherokee Nation of yours is a fascinating place to me. I've never seen anything like it.

14

I didn't know anyplace like it existed anywhere in the world. I thought that Indians were wild, you know?"

"I guess most white people believe that," said George.

"I was amazed when Mr. Peck and those other members of your council came up to Connecticut to interview me for my position here. I don't know what I was expecting when I heard where they were from, but I certainly wasn't expecting men in three-piece suits and top hats. A couple of them had dark skin, but other than that, they looked like — well, like white men."

"We've had a large mixed-blood population for a long time now," said George. "We're all citizens of the Cherokee Nation."

Lang took a sip of his coffee, then looked over the cup at George.

"Well, anyhow," he said, "it's a fascinating place."

"A little complicated at times too," said George. "You might be interested in the jurisdictional problems we have to face here. That gunfight you asked about, for example."

"Yes?"

Lang put his cup down and leaned forward, his elbows on the table.

"The United States government doesn't allow us jurisdiction over noncitizens. For instance, if you were to commit a crime while you're here in the Cherokee Nation, you would be

15

subject to federal law, not Cherokee law."

"Oh, really?"

"The white man we just threw in jail is over there right now yelling that we have no right to hold him. But as Captain Rider told him, a little knowledge of the law is dangerous. The man only knows what I just told you, that he's subject to federal law and not to Cherokee law. What he does not know is that the jurisdictional situation does not give him free rein to shoot up our streets. We can stop him, detain him, and turn him over to the federal authorities."

"I see," said Lang. "That's very interesting."

A waiter came and refilled the two cups, and George took a tentative sip of the fresh, hot coffee.

"I guess it is," he said. "It's gotten to where it's just everyday business to me. There are a lot of whites down here these days — more all the time, it seems, so we have to think about it all the time. But let's change the subject. Do you mind?"

"No, I don't mind. What would you like to talk about?"

"How's your job going?" George asked. "Any complaints yet?"

"The job's working out to be almost perfect," said Lang. "It seems almost too good to be true. I keep waiting for something to go wrong."

"Let's hope it doesn't. There's no reason

that things shouldn't go right for you."

"It's just so unusual to have no complaints," said Lang with a good-natured chuckle. "I'm getting along wonderfully with everyone on the faculty — well, almost everyone. There is one teacher of arithmetic about whom I have some . . . worries. Well, it's probably nothing. I shouldn't have mentioned it."

George thought for a moment about pursuing the subject, but it was obvious that Lang already thought he had said too much, so he let it go.

"What are your students reading right now?" he asked.

"Oh, we're into *Plutarch's Lives.* I've just assigned the life of Mark Anthony — Marcus Antonius, I should say. We're reading in Latin, of course."

"Of course," said George. They talked about Plutarch and about Cicero until George Tanner, reluctantly, said that he really should get back to the prison. Sheriff Go-Ahead Rider had been there alone for a while, and, after all, George was on duty and getting paid.

"I should go too," said Lang. "I've got some papers to mark before Monday's classes. Thank the sheriff for me, will you?"

"For what?" asked George.

"For allowing me the pleasure of your company for a few minutes."

They got up and walked to the counter,

where George paid for the coffee, and just as they turned to leave the café, a large man in a gray suit and bowler hat came through the door, bringing with him some of the cold air from outside.

"Well, hello, Mr. Winters," said Lang. "What a surprise. What brings you to Tahlequah?"

"Uh, business, Mr. . . . Lang, is it?"

"Yes, Christopher Lang. We met in Pennsylvania. I was on my way down here to —"

"Yes. Yes. Of course," said Winters. "How do you do? Well, excuse me, please. I'm in rather a hurry. Uh, business, you know."

Winters pushed his way abruptly past George and Lang. Then they stepped out onto the sidewalk and stood for a moment in the cold air, George looking through the window toward Winters.

"Real friendly fellow," he said.

"Yeah," said Lang. "Oh, we're not really friends. We just met once. That's all. Well, thank you for the coffee, George, and the conversation."

He held out his hand and George took it in his own.

"It was a pleasure, Chris," he said. "We'll do it again real soon."

The two friends then parted company, George headed for the jail, Lang going west toward his small home near the campus of the seminary.

—2—

George Tanner hung his hat and coat on the wall pegs just inside the office door. He walked the few steps over to the chair behind his small desk and sat down. Across the room, Rider was sitting behind his own desk, puffing his corncob pipe contentedly, leaning back, his feet propped up. His two Colt revolvers lay on the desktop side by side, handles out.

"You and old Lang have a good intellectual visit?" Rider asked.

George glanced up at Rider. He wondered if Rider was somehow scoffing at him, but if so, he couldn't see it in the sheriff's face.

"Yeah," he said. "We did. Chris Lang is a very bright fellow. A nice guy too. He took his degrees at the Hartford Seminary in Connecticut. It's a fine school, and I believe he took full advantage of it. We're lucky to have him here."

Rider grunted and puffed at his pipe. Thick clouds of bluish smoke drifted across the room, threatening to fill it from wall to wall and floor to ceiling.

"Rider," said George. "How come I get the feeling that you don't like Chris Lang? What is there not to like about him?"

"It ain't that, George," said Rider. "I don't even know him. You can't hardly not like someone you don't even know."

"What is it then?"

"Oh, nothing really. It's none of my business, I guess. I just wonder how come they have to go all the way to Connecticut to find a teacher. We send lots of Cherokees off to school. Ain't we got anyone right here who could have took that job?"

"Yeah, Rider, we do," said George, not trying to hide his exasperation. "But you pinned a badge on his chest his first day back from college. Remember?"

"You ain't the only Cherokee around with a college education, George," said Rider.

"Do you know of another one with a degree in the classics? Another one who can teach Greek and Latin?"

"I don't know nothing about that," said Rider. "But then, I ain't been looking for one; that ain't my job. I do wonder, though, if anyone ever really looked for a qualified Cherokee to fill that post. 'Course, I don't know what anyone needs Greek and Latin for anyhow. But like I said, it ain't none of my business."

"No, I don't suppose it is," said George. He felt himself getting a little hot under the collar. This conversation was beginning to shape itself into an argument, and George didn't really want to argue with Rider. He clenched his teeth.

"Just like it ain't none of my business that he seems to be taking up with Hannah Girty."

"Oh," said George, "I get it. You're afraid that Chris and Hannah might get serious about each other, might get married and start producing little halfbreeds, more people like me. Be careful: Your full-blood prejudice is showing, Rider."

"Now, I didn't say that. Don't go putting words in my mouth, George. I'm just wondering how old Willit's going to take it. That's all."

"Well, I, for one, am glad to have Chris Lang in Tahlequah and teaching at the seminary," said George. "Our students deserve the best they can get, and Chris is certainly one of the best. And it's nice to have someone around with whom it's possible to have an intelligent conversation now and then."

The deliberate jab of that last statement was not missed by Rider, but he didn't let it bother him. He knew that he had irritated George, and that George had to fight back. Rider would not have had any respect for him had he not.

Rider stood up, tucked his revolvers into his pants, and picked up a stack of papers off the top of his desk.

"I've got to go over to the capitol and see the judge," he said. "Other than them two gunfighters we just throwed in, there's only two prisoners left in the cells, old Cletus

Foot and Charlie McCoy. They're probably sobered up by now; you can let them go anytime you've a mind to. I'll be back directly."

He put on his hat, shouldered his coat, and left the office. George will cool off in a short while, Rider thought as he walked across the street. He supposed that he shouldn't have said anything about the teacher. He knew how George felt about the man, but he did resent the importation of white men for jobs that Cherokees could do as well.

And in spite of his denial to George Tanner, Rider admitted to himself that he did have a prejudice against mixed marriages, especially when the husband was white. It had nothing to do with race. Rider did not hate white men, but a Cherokee citizen raised by a white man almost always grew up with the sentiments of a white man.

Rider could easily foresee the time in the not too distant future when the mixed-blood citizens of the Cherokee Nation would outnumber the full-bloods and there would be very little difference between the mixed-bloods and the white intruders. Once a majority of Cherokees became for all practical purposes white, he thought, the days of the Cherokee Nation would be numbered, at least the Cherokee Nation as he knew it. It would be voted out of existence by its own citizens.

He stepped onto the square of the big brick capitol building, the structure that dominated the Tahlequah landscape, and he saw two young men — teenage boys, really — walking toward him. He knew them both, students at the Male Seminary.

"Howdy, boys," he said as they were about to pass him on the lawn. They stopped, hands in their back pockets, heads down.

"Hello, Sheriff Rider."

"How're your folks doing, Coley? I ain't seen them for a while."

"Oh, they're just fine, Sheriff," said Coley Fletcher. "At least, they were a couple of weeks ago when I last saw them. I ain't been up toward home since then."

"Yeah," said Rider. "It's a good long ride up there."

Coley Fletcher's father, Coyne, a prosperous mixed-blood citizen, was one of the biggest ranchers in the Cherokee Nation, running a vast herd of cattle over thousands of acres in the Cooweescoowee District. Under the laws of the Cherokee Nation, no individual could own land, but each citizen could use as much land as he could show need for as long as he didn't run over onto his neighbors' property, and he could own the improvements he made to that land. Coyne Fletcher had prospered under that system.

"Tommy," Rider said, turning to the other young man, a full-blood, "I saw your daddy just yesterday. He told me you're doing real well in school. He's sure proud of you."

"Thank you, sir," said Tommy Snail.

"Well, keep up the good work, boys," said Rider, and he started to walk on toward the capitol. Then he stopped and turned, calling out to Tommy Snail with a last thought.

"Tommy."

"Yes sir?"

"Do you boys study the classics?"

"Yes sir," said Tommy. "Both of us do."

Rider noticed that Coley ducked his head just a bit at that comment.

"Well?"

"Sir?"

"Well, how is it? Studying the classics?"

"Oh," said Tommy. "Well, sir, I think it's a very interesting subject, and Mr. Lang is an excellent teacher."

"Uh-huh," said Rider. "And what good do you reckon all that Greek and Latin is ever going to do you?"

"Well, I don't know," said Tommy. "I suppose it helps to sharpen one's mental faculties." He smiled and gave a shrug.

"I think it's all a bunch of shit," said Coley. "Myself, I'd rather be roping cows."

Rider hesitated. He looked at Coley, then at Tommy, and finally back at Coley. He nodded his head.

"Yeah," he said. "Yeah. I think so too, Coley. 'Course, probably you and me ain't as smart as Tommy there. See you boys around."

"Yeah," said Coley.

"See you, Sheriff," said Tommy.

Rider headed on toward the building, and the two students stood for a moment watching him go. When he was out of earshot, Coley picked up the conversation with Tommy that Rider had interrupted.

"Tommy," he said, and his voice was pleading, "my old man will beat the hell out of me if I don't pass this Latin course. You got to help me. You're my only chance. Hell, you're way up at the top of the class, boy. Come on now. What do you say?"

"I don't know what I can do, Coley," said Tommy. "I offered to study with you, but you put it off. You waited too late for this exam that's coming up. Maybe if you start studying with me now you'll be able to do better on the *next* exam and salvage some kind of grade out of the course, but the truth is I don't really see how you can do anything in only three or four days. You just waited too long. That's all."

"There's got to be a way."

"Listen, Coley. You'd better not try to copy off of me during the exam. Mr. Lang would be sure to see you, or even if he didn't spot you, he'd figure it out reading the papers, and then we'd both be kicked out of school. That wouldn't do you any good, and it would ruin me as well. So don't you try it.

You hear me? Don't you dare."

"Hell, I ain't that stupid," said Coley. "But there's got to be some other way. Damn it, Tommy, I just got to pass that damn thing."

Rider climbed the stairs inside the capitol and peeked into the judge's office. He could hear voices coming from the chief's office next door, but the door was nearly closed, so he couldn't see who was in there. He recognized the voice of Chief Ross, of course, but he couldn't quite place the other one.

"Bill," the other man was saying, "the pressures for the railroad interests are getting stronger all the time. I just don't know how much longer the council will be able to hold out."

"We have got to hold out," said the chief, William P. Ross. "We all know what the railroad can do to us. It will bring all manner of riffraff into our country. It's happened other places, and it will happen here too, if we don't stop them. But perhaps even worse than that for the future of our nation, it will almost for certain flood us with a noncitizen population. The railroad coming through the Cherokee Nation will be the beginning of the end."

Judge Boley looked up from his desk, and Rider's attention drifted away from the conversation he was inadvertently eavesdropping on. He had heard it all argued on both sides before anyhow.

"Rider," said the judge. "Come on in."

As the sheriff stepped into the judge's office, he jerked a thumb toward the conversation next door.

"Who's that in there with the chief?" he asked.

"It's Ira Peck," said Boley.

"The council meeting's over," said Rider. "They still worrying over that railroad issue?"

"The meeting didn't resolve anything," said Boley. "I'm not sure our council can do anything about it anyway. One of these days we're all going to have to face the fact that the U.S. government is going to do anything it wants to do to us, no matter what our council says. What can I do for you?"

Rider stepped up to the desk and handed the papers to the judge.

"Here's the chits on those old boys who have court dates," he said. "Most of them's for drinking. A couple got into fights."

The judge took them and heaved a sigh.

"Okay," he said. "I think I'll throw the book at them this time. I'm getting tired of this."

Christopher Lang stepped up to the front door of a modest house on a side street west of Muskogee Avenue. He gave a rap on the door, stepped back, and took off his hat. In a moment the door was opened by a plump, middle-aged Cherokee woman. She smiled when she saw Lang.

"Hello," she said in English that was obviously a second language for her. "Come in, Mr. Lang. Come in."

"Thank you, Mrs. Girty," said Lang, stepping through the doorway. "Is Hannah at home?"

"Yes. Come on and sit down. I get you some coffee."

Lang sat at the table. He reached down to put his hat on the floor beside his chair.

"Thank you very much," he said.

Just then Hannah came into the room. She was no more than eighteen years old and the picture of youthful health and beauty. Her skin was brown and smooth and her hair long, straight, and black. She smiled at Lang, and he thought that he would melt. Instead, he pushed back his chair and stood.

"Hello," he said, looking into the deepest, darkest eyes he had ever seen.

"Hi, Chris," she said, and she let him look into her eyes for only a few seconds before she cast them back down at the floor.

Mrs. Girty put a cup of coffee on the table in front of Lang.

"I thought that perhaps we could go for a walk," said Lang. "It's getting a little warmer outside. I think it's going to be a nice day."

"Sure," said Hannah, and then she glanced at her mother. "Okay?" she said.

"Okay," said Mrs. Girty.

"But drink your coffee first," said Hannah. "I'll have some with you."

Across the street behind a large old oak tree, Willit Barnes skulked and watched the Girty house. His eyes were full of jealous hatred. He was uneducated, but he was a hardworking young man. Hannah, he thought, was his girl. Though he himself was nearly white, he resented this white man coming down from the Northeast, from Yankee country, with his polished ways and his snotty education, and trying to take what belonged by rights to Willit. He wouldn't stand for it. By God, he would not.

—3—

Christopher Lang and Hannah Girty had not walked far down the road when a sharp voice from behind brought them to a halt.

"Hey, teacher."

The two stopped walking and turned almost together to look. There was Willit Barnes, standing spread-legged in the middle of the road. His fists were clenched, and he had a mean look on his face.

"Willit," said Hannah, "what are you up to?"

"You seem to know me," said Lang. "Just who are you?"

"The name's Willit Barnes, and don't you forget it."

"Willit," said Hannah, "don't you be starting any trouble here."

"He's the one looking for trouble," said Barnes. "I never asked him to come around here sparking my girl."

"I ain't your girl, Willit Barnes," said Hannah, in her excitement forgetting to watch her English usage, as she had been doing around Lang, "and I told you that already. You just go on out of here and leave us alone."

"I ain't going to do no such thing," said Barnes. "Everyone's laughing at me. Let a

Yankee schoolteacher steal my girl. Well, I ain't going to stand for it, and I mean it."

"Mr. Barnes," said Lang, taking a step toward this new adversary, "I'm not looking for any trouble with you. I don't even know you. But Hannah has her own mind, and if she wants to take a walk with me, I don't really see that it's any of your business."

"No? Well, I'm making it my business. Come on, teacher. Come on."

Barnes held his fists up and started walking to his left, as if he meant to circle Lang.

"Come on where?" said Lang.

"Come on and fight me," shouted Barnes. "What the hell did you think I meant? You think I meant take a walk with me? Come on, teacher. You afraid to fight?"

"Mr. Barnes, I really wish you wouldn't do this," said Lang.

"Come on, damn you."

"Willit, you better not. You better just get out of here right now," screamed Hannah.

Lang took off his hat and extended it toward Hannah. He shook his head a bit sadly.

"He's not going to listen to reason," he said. "I suppose I'll just have to oblige him."

Hannah took the hat in her hands and looked at Lang with wide eyes.

"You mean fight him?" she said.

Lang shrugged his way out of his jacket and handed it to her.

"If he insists."

"Oh no," said Hannah. "Chris? Willit?"

"Don't worry," said Lang. "Just step over there out of the way."

He struck a pugilistic stance and did a little dance. Barnes stopped circling for a moment and gave him a puzzled look. Then he stepped in and swung a wild roundhouse right. Lang blocked it neatly with his left arm and popped Barnes on the side of the head with a sharp right cross. Stunned, Barnes stepped back and rubbed the side of his face. He scowled and rushed forward, madder than before.

Lang danced aside, and Barnes rushed past him. He stopped and whirled and was met by a left jab to the nose. Another one quickly followed. Barnes stepped back again, wiped an arm across his face, and looked down at the blood on his shirtsleeve. He had been mad before — the man was courting his girl. Now he was furious, for the man was humiliating him in front of her.

"Do we have to go on with this, Mr. Barnes?" asked Lang.

Barnes looked up at Lang. He was panting and red-faced. He doubled his fists and raised them again.

"I'm going to kill you," he said, and he stepped forward, swinging wild. Lang blocked and ducked, then jabbed twice again. Both jabs hit their mark, and the second was followed by a hard right that sent Barnes sprawling in the dirt. His face was a bloody mess.

"I'm sorry," said Lang, looking down at the results of his handiwork, "but you're the one who pressed this fight. Are you all right?"

"Just leave me the hell alone," blubbered Barnes.

Lang reached for his hat and coat. "Let's go, Hannah," he said.

George Tanner had just finished his lunch at home. He daubed at his mouth with a napkin and pushed his chair back away from the table.

"Thank you, darling," he said. "That was a real fine lunch."

"I'm glad you liked it," said Lee Tanner, stepping in front of her husband to give him a fond kiss on the lips. George put his arms around her and held her close for a moment. Then he turned his head for a look at little Rider Tanner asleep in his crib.

"He sure is sleeping soundly," he said.

"He's a happy baby," said Lee. "And he's beautiful."

"He sure is," said George. "Just like his mother. Well, I'd better get back to work, even though I'd much rather stay here with the two people I love most in the whole world."

They indulged in one more fond kiss, and George broke away. He stepped to the door and reached for his hat and coat.

"George," said Lee. He had just put his hat on and had one arm in a sleeve of his coat.

"Yes?"

"George, why don't you ask Chris to come to dinner tonight? And ask him to bring Hannah Girty along with him if he wants to."

George finished getting into his coat and stepped over to give Lee another kiss.

"I think that's a great idea," he said. "I'll track him down and ask him."

"And the Riders too if they'll come," she added. "We'll have plenty to eat, and Captain Rider hasn't seen his little namesake for over a week now."

George hesitated at the door and wrinkled his brow.

"I don't know if Rider will want to come over here if he knows that Chris has been invited," he said.

Lee scowled. She knew about the near argument between George and Rider. George had told her that Rider was totally irrational when it came to the subjects of mixed marriages and whites being employed by the Cherokee Nation.

"Ask," said Lee.

"I'll ask."

Coley Fletcher hugged his coat close to his body and turned for the woods on the north end of town. He looked around furtively to see if he was being watched.

"Come on, Tommy," he said.

Tommy Snail followed him, and soon the two young men were hidden in the woods. Coley led the way a little farther until they came to a small clearing. He sat down on a flat rock and leaned back against a tree. Then he opened his coat and pulled out a bottle of whiskey. He uncorked the bottle and took a drink.

"Ah," he said, wiping his mouth with the back of his hand. He held the bottle out toward Tommy. "It's good. Have some."

"Coley, we could get in trouble for this," said Tommy.

"Aw, come on. Who's going to know? Have a swig."

Tommy took the bottle and drank from it, coughing and holding it back out toward Coley at the same time. "That burns," he said.

Coley laughed and took another drink. "That's what's good about it," he said. "It burns good." He took another swig and offered the bottle again to Tommy.

Tommy took it and sipped tentatively, then returned it to its owner. "Are we going to get drunk?" he said.

"Hell, I hope so. Quit worrying. Didn't you check out at school like I told you to?"

"Yeah, I checked out for the weekend. I told them I was going home."

"All right." Coley took another drink. "I got us a room at the hotel. No one's going to see us drunk. We'll just wait until after dark and go on down to the hotel and go into the room and sleep it off. That's all. Here. Have another drink."

Tommy took another tiny sip and handed the bottle back.

"Well," said Coley, taking another drink, "I've made up my mind."

"About what?"

"I'm going to break into Lang's office and steal the exam. That's what I'm going to do."

"You can't do that," said Tommy, astonished at Coley's brazen pronouncement.

"The hell I can't. You just hide and watch."

"Well — why bother?" said Tommy. "Even if you manage to cheat and get away with it and pass Mr. Lang's class, you're still flunking algebra. So what would you accomplish?"

"Ah, hell," said Coley, "that algebra class is no problem. All you got to do there is to just smile at old Morrison. That's all."

Tommy's face wrinkled as if he had just put something distasteful into his mouth.

"I'm going to break in and get that exam," said Coley, "and that's all there is to it."

"Well, don't ask me to go with you," said Tommy. "I'm not going to have anything to do with anything like that. That's just stupid."

"Hell, I ain't asking you. Did I ask you?" He drank again.

"No," said Tommy.

"And don't be calling me stupid."

"Well, it's a stupid *idea*," said Tommy. "Anyone can have a stupid idea." He paused for an uncomfortable moment. "Coley?"

"What?"

"You can't do it. You can't steal the exam."

"Why not?"

"When Mr. Lang sees that the exam is gone, he'll just make up another one. Besides that, he'll know that someone took it, and he'll be watching out for cheating. He'll be watching like a hawk."

Coley took another drink. He looked thoughtful for a long silent moment.

"I'll get in there at night when no one's around and I won't be interrupted," he said, "and I'll copy it. Then I can look up the answers before the test. That's what I'll do."

"It'll be dark in there at night. If you put on a light, someone might see it."

"Damn it," said Coley. He drank.

"Coley?"

"What?"

Tommy turned his back and walked a couple of steps away.

"No," he said. "I better not say it. I'm not going to help you. I shouldn't even be talking to you about this."

"What?" said Coley. "What were you going to say?"

"Nothing."

Coley got to his feet and ran over to stand beside Tommy. He held the bottle in front of Tommy's face. "Here," he said. "Have a drink. Go on."

Tommy took the bottle and drank from it.

"Go on," said Coley. "Go on. Have another."

Tommy did. It was getting a little easier with each swallow.

"Now," said Coley, "what were you going to say?"

"I better not."

"Damn it, Tommy, you already said you wouldn't go with me, and I never even asked you to do that, but if you've got an idea of how I can pull this off, you better tell me. We're friends, ain't we? You don't want to see me get killed, do you?"

Tommy took another drink and handed the bottle back to Coley.

"All right," he said. "If you're going to break in anyway, you could steal the exam, like you said, bring it over to the hotel room, and copy it there. Then you could go put it back."

Coley thought hard, letting the plan soak into his brain. He was already flush with the whiskey.

"That would mean breaking in twice," he said. "Two chances of getting caught."

"Not as much chance of getting caught as if you put a light on in the office at night and stayed in there long enough to copy the exam," said Tommy. "And you'd have to have a light on to read the exam and copy it."

"Yeah," said Coley. "Yeah. You're right. Okay. That's what I'll do. I'll break in twice. I'll go get it, take it to the hotel and copy it, and then go put it back. Just like you said."

George Tanner was sitting at his desk, and Rider at his. George looked up. Rider was busy with paperwork. George was trying to figure out how to ask Rider to join him and his family for dinner with Chris Lang and Hannah Girty. He imagined several possible Rider responses to the invitation. He looked back down at his desk and tried to appear to be busy. Then he shot another glance at Rider.

"George," said the sheriff, "you want to say something?"

"Oh. Yeah," said George. "I thought you were busy. I didn't want to bother you."

"I am busy," said Rider, "but I could see you fidgeting over there, and that bothered me. What is it?"

"Well, it's just that — Lee asked me to ask you if you and your family would like to join us for dinner this evening. That's all."

"Oh," said Rider.

"Well," said George, "that's not exactly all. That's the invitation. You're invited, and we'd like to have you, but . . ."

"But what, George?"

"Well, I'm also supposed to ask Chris Lang and Miss Girty to join us. That's all."

"That's a pretty good-sized crowd for dinner," said Rider.

"That's what Lee wants," said George with a shrug. "A dinner party, I guess. She said we're going to have plenty to eat."

Rider leaned back in his chair and put his feet up on the desk.

"Well, thank you, George," he said. "It sounds like it might be real nice."

"Does that mean you'll come?"

"Sure," said Rider. "I'm looking forward to it already. Your wife is a fine cook, and I ain't seen little Rider for a spell."

George looked at Rider for a moment. The man was a constant puzzle to him. He stood up and walked to the peg for his hat.

"Do you mind if I go out for a few minutes?"

"No," said Rider. "Go ahead."

"I have to hunt up Chris and tell him."

"Do you know where he's at?"

"Well, no."

"Take a horse out of the barn if you want to," said the sheriff. "You might have to ride around a bit to find him."

"Thanks, Rider," said George. "I will." He put on his hat, took his coat, and walked out the door, shaking his head.

—4—

It was crowded in the Tanner house that evening, but Lee had planned well and made room for all. The six adults had places around the table, and the two Rider children, Tootie and Buster, had been provided with their own special place, a wide plank placed across two wooden crates and covered by a white tablecloth. The children sat on the floor beside the makeshift table. There was plenty of food, and everyone was enjoying the meal.

"By the way," said Lang, speaking to Rider, "from what George explained to me about your jurisdictional situation here, you may want to hold me for the United States marshal."

Rider looked up at Lang. He finished chewing and swallowed before he spoke.

"How's that?" he asked.

"Well," said Lang, "I assume that brawling in the streets is some kind of violation, although I was only defending myself."

"What happened?" said George.

"Chris did try to walk away from it several times," said Hannah. "He even tried to talk Willit out of it, but Willit wouldn't listen.

41

He's so hardheaded."

"Willit?" said George. "Willit Barnes?"

"Suppose you tell us what happened," said Rider.

"Well," said Lang, "Hannah and I were walking down the street near her house, when this . . . Willit Barnes stepped out into the road behind us and called out to me. He didn't call me by name. He called out, 'teacher.' He accused me of trying to steal his girl and said he wanted to fight me."

"I told him I didn't belong to him or anyone else," said Hannah. "I told him to go away and leave us alone."

By this time everyone was listening. All eyes in the room, even those of the Rider children, were on Lang. All eyes in the room were on Lang, that is, except those of little Rider Tanner, who was quiet in his crib. Sheriff Rider glanced across the table at George.

"I was afraid something like this would happen. Go on," he said to Lang.

"Well," said Lang, "there's really not much more to tell. He wouldn't listen to reason. Instead he moved toward me with his fists up, so I prepared to defend myself. After he took a swing at me, I punched him a few times, and that was about it."

"You should've seen Chris," said Hannah. "He was great. Why, his fists moved so fast, he hit Willit two or three times before Willit could even try to swing again."

"You sure don't look like a man who's just been in a fistfight," said George. "You seem to have a talent you've neglected to tell me about."

"Willit never laid a hand on him," said Hannah.

"I just thought that since you two are the law around here, you might want to know about it," said Lang. "I did leave him lying there in the street — a little bloody."

"Well, I don't believe we'll need to hold old Chris here in jail, George," said Rider. "Do you?"

"Oh, no," said George, a smile on his face, "I don't think so."

"In fact," said Rider, "old Elwood Lovely would likely laugh me out of town if I was to send for him all the way over here for just a fistfight."

"Elwood Lovely?" said Lang.

"He's the deputy United States marshal over at Muskogee," said George. "He's the closest one to us here in Tahlequah."

"Oh," said Lang. "Well, if he should decide he wants me, George knows where to find me."

"But that's not all," said Hannah, her voice and her face expressing concern.

"Well then, what more is there, Hannah?" asked Rider.

"Willit said he was going to kill Chris."

"Is that a fact?" asked Rider. George

couldn't tell if Rider was being serious or feigning seriousness.

"He was just angry," said Lang. "In fact, I think I had already bloodied his nose by the time he said that. I wouldn't worry about it."

"You don't know Willit," said Hannah. "You don't know him like I do. If he's mad enough, he *could* kill someone. And he was real mad at Chris."

"She's right, Chris," said George. "I should at least go and have a talk with him." He glanced at Rider. "Right?"

"Oh, yeah, George," said Rider. "Why don't you do that in the morning."

"On Sunday morning?" asked George.

"We go to church, Captain Rider," said Lee.

"Oh yeah. Sure. I wasn't thinking about that. Well, look him up right after church. That'll be soon enough."

There was a sudden lull in the conversation as they all turned their attention back to their plates. After he had taken a bite, then chewed and swallowed it, Lang spoke up again.

"I apologize, ladies, for bringing up the previous conversation," he said. "It wasn't proper talk over a meal. I should have realized that it would lead to more detail than I had intended. I should have waited until we were finished eating. The meal is delicious, by the way, Lee. I want to thank you for inviting us."

"It's our pleasure," said Lee. "Your presence

in town has been wonderful for George. Are we ready for coffee? Anyone?"

"Sure," said Rider.

"Rider's always ready for coffee," said George. "I guess I will too. Chris? Hannah?"

They all answered in the affirmative, and Lee went after the pot and the cups.

"Me too," said Buster from the small table. Lee gave Rider's wife Exie a questioning look.

"It's okay," said Exie. "Rider gives it to him at home all the time anyway."

"Can I have some too?" asked Tootie.

Just then little Rider made some complaining noises from his crib.

"Oh dear," said Lee.

"Go ahead," said George. "I'll get him."

Rider stood up first and moved toward the crib. "Keep your seat," he said. "Let me take care of little Rider. I ain't seen him for a while anyhow. And I think he was just calling out for me. I recognized that noise he made."

He picked up the baby and held him close to his face. "Little Rider," he said, talking in Cherokee, "you don't have to cry. Here's old Rider come to see you. You know me? You remember me?"

The baby seemed to calm down, and Rider laid him up on his shoulder, holding him close in his left arm and patting his back with his right hand. He stayed on his feet and paced the floor. Little Rider seemed quite content.

Lee poured coffee all around, put away the pot, and moved over beside Rider.

"You want me to take him so you can drink your coffee?" she asked.

"No," said Rider. "We're doing just fine, us Riders."

"Well, Chris," said George, "you had a real interesting day, didn't you. Between seeing that fellow you knew from Pennsylvania and your fight with Willit Barnes."

"Yes, I suppose it was an eventful day," said Lang, "but this evening is the most memorable part of it."

"Thank you," said Lee.

"Someone from Pennsylvania's in town?" asked Rider.

"I don't really know him," said Lang, taking a sip of coffee and putting the cup back down. "His name is Winters. I met him while I was coming down here with Councilman Peck. We stopped in Philadelphia along the way, and Mr. Peck had a brief meeting with him. I gathered they were business associates of some kind."

"Oh, yeah," said Rider. "I knew old Peck had a partner back east somewhere. I guess he's come down to check on the store."

"Is anyone ready for pie?" asked Lee.

Coley Fletcher was in the bushes at the edge of the seminary campus. He had left Tommy back in the room at the hotel.

46

Tommy had been too scared to go with him, but that was all right, Coley thought; he'd probably just get in the way. Besides that, Tommy seemed a bit drunk. He couldn't really handle the whiskey like Coley could. Coley had drunk quite a bit, but he knew that he was all right. Hell, he was used to it.

The campus was dark. The only light Coley could see was in old Broom's room. Broom was a kind of caretaker and all-around maintenance man. Coley figured that he was probably asleep.

There were no lights on in the rooms where the kids who hadn't gone home for the weekend were sleeping; the housemaster on duty had already put them out. Everyone was asleep. Coley had planned it that way. That was the reason he had waited so late into the night. He stood up and made a run for the building.

Panting, he leaned against the red brick wall of the big building. It was even bigger than the capitol, but it was not right in town, so the two buildings did not compete with each other for attention.

Coley waited a long moment for any sign that anyone had seen him. Everything was quiet. Off in the darkness a hoot owl sounded, disturbing the night. Coley shivered. A hoot owl was supposed to be an ominous sign, but Coley didn't believe in that stuff. He dismissed as foolish superstition what the full-bloods thought about it. Still, when it sounded again, Coley felt goose bumps form all over his body.

He started moving along the wall toward the window of Lang's office, happy that it was on the ground floor. There was a bright moon shining, and he hurried from the shade of one tree or bush to another. At Lang's window, though, there was no shade. If anyone happened along, Coley knew, he would be seen. He had to hurry.

He reached up and tested Lang's window, and to his relief, he found it unlocked. He raised it easily. Then he scampered up and over the windowsill and dropped to the office floor inside. Quickly he turned around on his knees and peered out over the edge of the sill. He saw no one, no sign that anyone had seen him. Everything was still and quiet.

He reached up and slowly pulled the window back down. If anyone saw it open, they might suspect that something was wrong. He went to the door that opened out onto the hallway and stood and listened for a moment. Then, hearing nothing, he moved to the desk. It was covered with papers and books. Damn, he thought; I wonder how much of this shit I'll have to look through to find that exam.

He shuffled through some of the papers on top of the desk, then picked one up and strained to read it. He moved to the window and held it up in the moonlight. It was Greek, he thought. He took it back and looked some more.

"Damn it," he said out loud. He sat down in Lang's chair and opened a desk drawer. He found a book like a ledger and opened it up. Turning and holding it up just right, he could tell that it was the teacher's grade book. He took it to the window and read his name and saw the low marks that went with it. He thought about changing them but realized that would be a stupid thing to do.

He returned to the desk, put the ledger back, and shut the drawer. Then he opened another, and there he found it: the Latin exam for Wednesday. It had to be. He took it to the window and read it in the light. He knew it was the exam. He went back to the desk and shut the drawer. He carefully tucked the exam into his coat, then went to the window.

Looking out, he could see no one. He slowly raised the window, looked again, and climbed out. He stood a moment, but all was silent, all except the owl in the woods. He turned around and pulled the window down, and then he ran.

Tommy Snail was asleep, and when the knock on the door woke him up, he jumped. For an instant, he couldn't remember where he was. Then it came back to him, and he hurried to the door.

"Coley?" he said in a harsh whisper.

"Open up," said Coley.

Tommy opened the door and Coley rushed in. He was already unfastening his coat.

"I got it," he said. "I got the son of a bitch."

He pulled out the paper and slapped it down on the table. Tommy hurried over to the other side of the room.

"I don't even want to see it," he said.

"That's all right," said Coley. "You don't have to see it. You don't have to do nothing."

He pulled out the chair and sat down at the table. There in front of him was the stolen exam, a stack of writing paper, a pen, and a bottle of ink. The whiskey bottle was also there. Together, the boys had not yet drunk half its contents. Coley picked it up and put it to his lips. He took a big swallow, put the bottle back on the table, and wiped his mouth with his sleeve.

"All right," he said. "Here we go," and he began to adjust the papers in front of him for comfortable writing. He dipped the pen in the ink and started to copy. From across the room, Tommy watched nervously. Coley was a slow writer, and it was agonizing for Tommy to watch. He wondered just how long the whole process would take.

He wished that he had really gone home for the weekend. He wished that he had not let Coley talk him into going with him to drink whiskey. He wished that he were somewhere else, and he even wished that he had never met Coley Fletcher.

Coley could talk him into just about anything, and he always seemed to have money for whatever he wanted to do. That was because Coley's father was rich, and always gave Coley money, as much as he wanted. And it had been especially easy for Coley to talk Tommy into spending this particular weekend with him in this way, because Tommy had not had the money for a train ride home, and he sure didn't want to spend a weekend at the school. Especially not now.

Coley put his pen down and took another drink.

"Coley," said Tommy.

"What?"

"You'd better hurry up and get that done. Don't forget, you've got to go all the way back over there again tonight to put it back. Otherwise, the whole plan will be wasted."

"Don't worry, Tommy," said Coley, dipping his pen into the ink bottle. "I'll get it done, and I'll put it back, and no one will ever be the wiser."

—5—

Mr. Forbes Winters stood in the alley behind the National Hotel. In dark shadow, he leaned against the back wall of the building, beside the rear door. The night had grown cold again, and Winters's breaths came out in visible puffs that slowly drifted away and dissipated like smoke. He wore a heavy great-coat, which added to his already considerable girth, the collar pulled up around his neck, his hands thrust deep into the big side pockets.

He had not waited long, though the cold night air made it seem longer than it had actually been, when he heard footsteps coming down the dark alley. He noticed that his palms were sweating, in spite of the temperature. He glanced toward his left and saw the shadowy outline of another man approaching. That man too wore a long coat. His head was covered by a wide-brimmed hat and he ducked against the cold air as he walked straight toward the spot where Winters waited. Winters felt his heart pounding in his chest. Stepping up close, the man stopped. Both men raised their heads slightly and looked into the other's eyes.

"Good evening, Councilman," said Winters, trying hard not to reveal the tremendous relief he felt at recognizing Ira Peck.

"Mr. Winters," said Peck, "let's get right to the point. It's damned chilly out here tonight. What did you need to see me about?"

"We may have a problem, Mr. Peck," said Winters. "That schoolteacher you had along with you when we last met in Philadelphia —"

"Lang," said Peck.

"Yeah. Lang. He saw me today, and he recognized me and called me by name. He'll remember the circumstances under which we met."

"Damn," said Peck. "I never considered that he would see you again, especially down here. Why didn't they send someone else?"

"They didn't, and he's seen me, and that's what matters," said Winters. "If he says anything to anyone else that puts the two of us together, your usefulness to us will have come to an end. This business is too important to let something botch it up now. There's a hell of a lot of money at stake here."

"Yes," said Peck. "I'm well aware of that. Why else would I have let myself get mixed up in this with you? Look. Why don't I have a talk with Mr. Lang and just tell him to keep his mouth shut. I'll tell him that it's a matter of internal Cherokee politics, and that if he lets on to anyone that he's seen us together, it will embarrass me politically. He

53

owes me at least that much for his job."

"You feel like you can depend on his word for that?" asked Winters.

"I think so."

"You'd damn well better be certain," said Winters. "Forget about what me and my people want. Just remember what exposure would mean to your career, not to mention your pocketbook. If he won't listen to reason, if you can't trust him to keep his mouth shut something else will have to be done — if it's not too late already."

Upstairs in the room that Coley Fletcher had rented, Tommy Snail had finally fallen asleep. Coley was barely able to keep his own eyes open, but he was still busy laboriously copying the Latin exam he had taken from the desk drawer of Christopher Lang. He was desperate to pass the exam, and he knew that he had to get back to the campus and replace it in the desk drawer in order to keep Lang from becoming suspicious.

His head dropped, and he brought it back up with a jerk, opening his eyes wide. He shook his head, trying to clear it. He reached for the whiskey bottle and realized that he had already emptied it of its contents.

"Damn," he said.

He picked up the pen and dipped it in ink to resume his work. Slowly, almost painfully, he copied the strange words. The tip of his tongue was protruding from one side of his otherwise tightly closed mouth, and his brow was deeply knit. He thought about stopping. He was very tired. But then he thought about Coyne Fletcher, the father who wanted so desperately to see him succeed, the man he was most afraid of in the whole world.

He dipped the pen again and continued writing. Twice more he fell asleep, and each time the dropping of his head brought him back around. At last he was done. The work was messy, but he could read it. He looked at the original exam. Luckily, he had not dirtied it much. Lang would probably never notice anything wrong with it. Now all he needed to do to finish the entire task was to replace the exam. He felt a tremendous sense of relief.

He pushed back the chair and stood on unsteady feet, feeling his head reel. God, I'm tired, he thought. I'll lay down for a few minutes and get some rest. Just a little rest. Then I'll take it back over there. He walked to the bed and fell heavily across it. The bouncing mattress failed to awaken Tommy, and soon Coley was in a deep sleep as well.

Sunday morning, Rider went down the road from his house on the bluff overlooking Tahlequah. He went to check on his two remaining prisoners, Orren Harkey and Bob Avery. The fire in the stove had gone down during the night, and a chill had settled inside the stone building. Rider got some wood and built up a good blaze in the firebox. Then he went to visit the cells. He stopped first outside the cell that housed Avery.

"Morning, Bob," he said. "I hope the night air helped cool you off some."

"Let me out of here, you son of a bitch," said Avery. "I'm a white man. You can't keep me in this damn Indian jail. It's against the law."

"I can't arrest you, Avery," said Rider, "but when you threaten lives in my jurisdiction, I can sure as hell lock you up and hold you for the federal authorities."

"The hell you can!"

"I've already sent a message over to Muskogee to the marshal's office. They'll be sending someone over to pick you up. Likely tomorrow. So you might as well settle down for a wait. You ain't going nowhere until they come by to pick you up."

"Well, you ain't got no right to freeze me to death in here while I'm waiting, do you?"

"I just stoked up the fire," said Rider. "It'll warm up directly. Wrap yourself up in that blanket for now, if you're that cold."

"I don't want to sit here like no damn blanket-ass Indian," said Avery.

"Suit yourself," said Rider, and he walked away from the cell, heading on down the row.

"Hey," shouted Avery, "I'm starving to death. When do we eat?"

"In good time," said Rider, walking on without looking back. He went to the stairs and climbed up to the second floor, where Harkey was locked up. He had purposely put the two men on different floors to keep them from yelling at each other. He sure didn't want to listen to that. As he approached the cell, Harkey sprang up from the cot and rushed to the door, clutching one of the bars in each hand.

"Rider," he said. "Rider, you going to let me out?"

"Not just yet," said the sheriff. "I can't do nothing for you on Sunday. You'll have to wait in here till sometime tomorrow."

"What for? I was just defending myself. I told you."

"Well, Orren," said Rider, "ordinarily I'd have to agree with you that a man's got a right to defend himself, but all we've got to go on as to how that fight got started is your word. The judge will have to sort all that out. And then there's another matter."

"What's that?"

"You know it's against the law for you to be carrying a gun in town."

"What?" said Harkey. "Against the law? I didn't know that. Hell. How's a man supposed to defend himself if he ain't got no gun on him? If I hadn't had my gun on me yesterday old Avery would have killed me for sure."

"In that case," said Rider, "we wouldn't have all these other details to worry about. All I'd have to do is hold Avery for old Elwood Lovely to take and charge with murder. That would have been a whole lot simpler for me. You too. By the way, did you know that Avery could press federal charges on you for shooting at a white man?"

"No. Does he know that?"

"I didn't tell him," said Rider. "Anyhow, the marshal's office will have to straighten it all out. It's out of my hands."

Tommy Snail opened his eyes slowly and reached up with one hand to rub the grit out of them. He squinted at the light coming in the window. His head hurt a little, and his stomach was growling from hunger. He did not feel well rested, but he was awake. He rolled his head to one side and saw Coley Fletcher lying there beside him asleep. Both students were still fully dressed, and their clothes were badly rumpled.

Tommy sat up slowly on the side of the bed. He moaned the moan of a man who is waking up the morning after a long, hard night. He held his head in both of his hands for a moment. Then he stood up and stretched. He walked over to the window and looked out onto Muskogee Avenue. There he could see the buggies of men and women dressed in their Sunday best on their way to church.

He walked across the room to the small table that held a bowl and a pitcher of water, and he poured some water into the bowl, then leaned over and splashed his face. He felt for the towel, picked it up, and dried his face and hands. Then he looked back at Coley, still sleeping.

I should have gone home for the weekend, he thought. Now what am I going to do with myself while he's lying there asleep? He glanced over at the desk where Coley had been working the night before and noticed that the bottle was empty. He might be asleep all day, he thought. Tommy knew that he had had only a few swallows, sips really, from the bottle. Coley had drunk almost all of it.

He was hungry. He checked his pockets to see if he had enough money on him for a breakfast somewhere, but he did not. Coley would have some, he thought, but he hesitated to wake Coley. Besides that, he and Coley both looked pretty rugged, and Tommy wasn't at all sure that he wanted to be seen out in public like that.

He wondered if he could make his way back to his room at school to get some fresh clothes. But what would he say if anyone saw him? He did not want to be seen at the school, especially if Mr. Morrison was on duty. He had checked out on Friday, telling them that he would be going home for the weekend. Maybe he could make up some excuse having to do with his family. But he couldn't think of anything that would make any sense, and he couldn't think of any way he could get into the building to get his clothes without being seen. Tommy had never been any good at telling lies. He was stuck.

He looked at Coley, lying there dead to the world, feeling no pain, suffering no anxiety. It wasn't fair. It was all Coley's fault. Coley had talked him into lying about the weekend in the first place. Then Coley had bought the whiskey. Now because of Coley, Tommy was bored and hungry in a hotel room in Tahlequah, and it was early Sunday morning. There was no place to go, and even if there had been, Tommy didn't have any money and wasn't fit to go out in public.

He glanced over again at the empty bottle on the desk, a scowl on his face. And he noticed the papers, Coley's copy of the exam. Tommy felt guilty just being in the same room with the copy. He started to look away, but something caught his eye and pulled his gaze back to the desktop. He took the few steps to the desk quickly and looked down at the papers.

There was Coley's clumsy copy, and there beside it, the original exam. Tommy felt a panic rise up from deep inside him. He ran over to the bed and grabbed Coley by the shoulders and shook him violently.

"Wake up," he shouted. "Coley! Wake up!"

"What? What the hell? Leave me alone. Get your goddamned hands off me, you creep."

Tommy jumped back, frightened. "Wake up, Coley, damn you!" he shouted, and he felt guilty for the language he used, but it was too late, he had already said it. It was Coley's bad influence on him, combined with Coley's dishonesty and foolishness, that had caused him to swear that way. "Wake up."

Coley at last opened his eyes. He looked into Tommy's face, puzzled.

"Tommy?" he said. "Oh. It's you." He sat up on the bed.

"Well, who'd you think it was?"

"Oh, just — someone. Never mind who. What's wrong with you anyhow? Is something wrong?"

"Look," said Tommy, pointing wildly toward the window. "Look. It's daylight. It's Sunday morning."

"So what?" said Coley. "You wake me up screaming at me like that just to tell me it's Sunday morning? Goddamn, buddy. Oh, my head. I wish you hadn't woke me up like that. If you'd have let me sleep just a little longer, I'd have slept it off. That's the way you have to do when you drink whiskey, Tommy. You have to sleep it off. Then when

61

you get up, you'll be all right, you won't have no hangover. But you got to get enough sleep. That's the whole secret. Damn. You've got a lot to learn."

"Well, I don't think I want to learn any more from you, Coley," said Tommy. "It's Sunday morning."

"You said that already," said Coley. "So what?"

Tommy stalked over to the desk and slapped his hand down on the exam.

"You didn't take it back," he shouted. "It's right here. You didn't go put it back like you said you would. Now what are you going to do?"

Coley stood up slowly and walked over to the desk. He looked down at the stolen exam, and he remembered that he had meant to lie down for only a short rest. He had meant to get up in a few minutes and return to the campus to replace the exam. Obviously, he had fallen asleep and stayed that way. As Tommy had so rudely informed him, it was Sunday morning. He stared at the offending paper there on the top of the desk.

—6—

"You left it here," said Tommy. "You left it right here all this time. Right here in this room. Why didn't you take it back like you said? Huh? Why didn't you? You were supposed to put this back where you got it last night. What are we going to do now?"

"All right," said Coley. "All right. Just calm down and let me think, will you? Let me think this thing out. All right? I'll come up with something."

He went over and sat down on the edge of the bed, wrinkling his face in serious and seemingly painful thought.

"Well?" said Tommy, following him. "Well, what are you going to do? You can't go back over there now. It's daylight."

"Shut up and let me think," said Coley. "How can I think with you yelling at me?"

Tommy's face took on a deep pout. "Well, all right," he said, "but I'm leaving. I've had enough of you and your ideas. I've had all of you I can take. I'm getting out of here right now, and nothing you can say to me will make any difference. Not now. Not anymore."

He reached for the doorknob, turned it, and found the door locked. He turned to get the key off of the table.

"Wait a minute," said Coley. "Hold on there, buddy. Think about it. Just where do you think you're going to go? Huh? Where you going?"

"I'll go home. That's where I should have gone in the first place. I should have gone home Friday, like I said I was doing. I shouldn't have lied. Lying always leads to trouble. Lying and drinking whiskey and stealing and cheating — all in one day. How did I ever let you talk me into this?"

He picked up the key and stuck it in the keyhole.

"Hell," said Coley, "by the time you get on out to your home way out there by Hulbert, walking the whole way, it'll be time to turn around and head back in. How you going to explain that to your folks? If you even make it that far. If you don't lay down and freeze to death in a ditch along the way."

"It's not that cold," said Tommy, but he thought about how cold it really was. It would be an awfully long and cold walk home. And if he left the hotel room, there would be no place else for him to go. His eyes started to sting, and he was afraid that he would cry. He sure didn't want Coley to see him cry, but he was so angry and upset that he was afraid it would happen anyway.

"Just take it easy," said Coley. "Calm down, will you? Relax. You ain't going to get in no trouble. Not over what I done. Hell, even if I was to get caught, which I ain't, I'd tell them you didn't have nothing to do with it. Why would you? Your grades are good. Hey. You're my good buddy. I ain't going to get you in no trouble. I promise. Trust me. Okay?"

Tommy stood by the door, hesitant and unsure. Coley was right. He couldn't go home now, and neither could he return to the campus. Either way, he would have too much to try to explain. Either way, he would be caught in a lie.

"All right," said Coley. "Listen. I got it. I got it figured out. It's only Sunday. Right? We got one more night. I'll go out there after dark tonight and put the exam back where I got it. Then when Lang shows up for work Monday morning, everything'll be fine. Okay?"

Tommy stood looking down at the floor, a serious sulk on his face.

"I don't know," he said. "What if Mr. Lang goes to his office for something today?"

"Well, I'll just have to hope and pray that he don't," said Coley. "That's all."

"Maybe he won't," said Tommy, trying desperately to be a little more positive about his predicament.

"Of course he won't," said Coley. "Besides, where you going to go if you don't stick with me? Huh? You got any other ideas? Come on. Let's go out, and I'll buy you a breakfast. Okay?"

"Okay," said Tommy, for he really had no idea what else he could do.

When the Tanner family stepped out the front door of the church following services, a cold thin rain was falling. It looked like the kind that could easily turn to sleet or even snow.

"Oh no," said Lee.

"Wrap that blanket real good around little Rider," said George. "Here. Let me help you." He took the baby and held him up while Lee adjusted the blanket.

"George," someone called. "Hey, George. Over here."

George looked over his shoulder out toward the road. A covered surrey stood in front of the church. George leaned over, trying to see who it was under there calling his name. Lee bent her knees to lower her gaze.

"It's Captain Rider," she said. She pulled the blanket up over the baby's head, and added, "Come on, George."

George took hold of Lee's arm, and they ran together to the surrey and climbed in.

"What is this, Rider?" said George.

"I figured you all had walked to church," said Rider, giving a flick of the reins. The surrey started forward with a lurch. "You do every Sunday. When I seen it start to rain like this, I figured I'd better come and get you. I couldn't have little Rider getting all cold and wet, could I? He might catch a cold or something."

"Well, it's awfully good of you, Rider," said Lee. "Thank you so much."

"Yeah," said George. "Thanks."

A buggy passed them, going in the opposite direction, and Rider waved and greeted the driver and passenger. He drove the rest of the few blocks to the Tanner house and pulled up in front.

"Thanks again," said Lee. "Will you come in for a cup of coffee?"

"No. I better not," said Rider. "Exie's probably holding lunch for me right now. I do appreciate the offer, though."

The Tanners climbed out of the surrey and hurried to their front door. Lee took the baby inside quickly, but her husband paused and looked back toward the surrey.

"Rider," he called out.

"What is it?"

"I'll be going out looking for Willit Barnes in a little while. If it's all right, I'll be getting a horse out of the sheriff's barn."

"Old Barnes lives over in Dog Town, don't he?" asked Rider.

"Yeah. I think so."

"Then you better take yourself a horse. See you later, George."

"Okay," said George as Rider got the surrey moving again. Then louder, he called out, "Thanks a lot, Rider," and he ducked on into the house.

Lee was still holding the baby in his blanket. George took off his hat and coat and hung them up, then went to her side. "Here," he said, "let me take him so you can get out of your coat." Lee handed little Rider to her husband and started to remove her coat and scarf. "There," said George. "There now. How's my boy? Huh? How you doing there, little Rider Tanner?"

"George," said Lee, "wasn't it thoughtful of Captain Rider to pick us up like that?"

"Yeah. It was, but I guess I'd better find a way to get us our own horse and buggy. We can't have Rider chasing after us like that every time the weather changes."

"No," Lee agreed, "we can't. He does too much for us already. He and Exie. They're certainly wonderful people, and the best friends anyone could ever hope for."

"Well," said George, "I'll get us a horse and buggy just as soon as I can."

After he finished his meal, George Tanner wrapped his coat around himself, pulled his hat down tight on his head, and walked the short distance from his house to the jail. He saw the surrey standing out on the street in front, so he went into the office before heading for the barn. Rider was there with a good fire burning in the stove.

"Working on Sunday, huh?" said George.

"We got two prisoners, George," said Rider. "Besides, Sunday's just another day as far as I'm concerned."

"Uh-huh," said George. "I'll bet that a whole bunch of preachers have worked real hard over the years trying to convert you."

"There's a few that ain't quit trying yet."

George chuckled.

"But speaking of the prisoners," he said, "do you suppose Elwood Lovely will get over here tomorrow to pick up Avery?"

"He probably will. Either that or send someone. He's usually pretty prompt."

George nodded his head toward the surrey.

"Do you think that was proper use of sheriff's equipment? Driving the surrey to pick me and my family up after church?"

"Oh," said Rider, filling his pipe bowl, "I reckon it is. You going on out to the barn now?"

"Yeah. I thought I'd saddle myself a horse and ride on out to Dog Town," said George. "I might as well get this over with."

"Why don't you drive the surrey out there and put it away for me while you're at it."

"Be glad to. After all, you got it out for my sake."

"For little Rider," said the sheriff, "and for Lee. I'd have let you walk in the rain."

"Yeah," said George. "That's what I meant."

"And George."

"Yes?"

"Be careful over there in Dog Town. Some of those folks don't give a damn about a badge on a man's chest."

"Don't worry," said George. "I'm just going to have a little talk with Willit. That's all. If I can even find him."

"And watch out for his old man," said Rider. "Old Barnes is a mean one." He stood up suddenly and reached for his two Colts on the desk. "Maybe I better ride along with you," he said.

"Rider," said George, "relax. I can take care of myself. I've learned a few things since I came to work for you, and I'm only going over there to have a talk with him, that's all. It's not as if I was going to try to arrest him."

Rider hesitated, his hands on the butts of his Colts, his pipe stem clamped in his teeth. He reached up and took the pipe out of his mouth, releasing a cloud of smoke into the air.

"All right, George," he said. "Go on. If I ain't here at the office when you get back, stop by the house. Will you?"

"I'll see you," said George, and he walked out the door.

Tommy Snail was finishing up a second helping of fried potatoes. He had already eaten two eggs, one heap of potatoes, and a big slice of ham. Across the table from him, Coley Fletcher had eaten almost as much. Their cups had just been refilled with hot coffee for the fourth time. Tommy was feeling better. No matter how bad things seemed, he thought, a good meal always made the world look a whole lot better.

He still wished that he had fresh clothes, and he was still convinced that he had been a fool to stay in town for the weekend with Coley. But a good meal under his belt made a big difference, and on top of that, Coley was paying for it.

Tommy glanced up when he heard the door open, and he saw George Tanner, the deputy sheriff, come walking in. The sight of the lawman made him nervous. He told himself that the deputy sheriff would not be out looking for Mr. Lang's missing Latin exam. That was only a concern of the faculty and administration of the seminary, a matter of school discipline. Or was it? After all, in order to get the exam, Coley had broken into the office of Mr. Lang. The law could be looking for the guilty party after all. And Tommy felt guilty by association.

He finished his potatoes and picked up the cup for a sip of coffee. The deputy sheriff was still standing just inside the door, looking around.

"I wonder who he's looking for," said

Tommy in a low voice.

"Who?" said Coley. He twisted in his chair to take a look. Then he turned back around. "Oh. Tanner? Hell. Who knows? He's probably looking for drunks. That's about all the sheriff's office does around here, ain't it? Lock up drunks?"

"I guess."

"Oh, say. He ain't making you nervous, is he?"

"No," Tommy lied. "I'm not nervous. I was just wondering. That's all."

"Well," said Coley, "we ain't got nothing to worry about from him. Watch this."

"Coley," Tommy protested, but Coley was already up on his feet and walking toward George. Tommy wanted to go out the back door, but he decided that he'd better sit still and hope for the best.

"Howdy, Mr. Tanner," said Coley. "You all right today?"

"I'm just fine, Coley," said George.

Casually, Coley dug some cash out of his pocket and laid it on the counter.

"Sam," he called out. "I'm ready to pay up here." Waiting for Sam, Coley turned back toward George. "Looking for someone?"

"You haven't seen Willit Barnes around town today, have you?" asked George.

Coley looked thoughtful for a moment, then turned his head toward where Tommy sat several tables away and raised his voice.

"Tommy," he said, "you seen old Willit Barnes around anywhere?"

"No," said Tommy in a barely audible voice.

"Thanks," said George, turning to leave.

"Has old Willit got himself in some kind of trouble?" asked Coley.

"No," said George. "I need to talk to him about something. That's all. See you around."

He went back outside and mounted his horse. He had stopped by the café because it was one of the few businesses open on a Sunday. He hadn't really expected to see Willit Barnes in there, but he had looked in just in case. It was a lot closer than Dog Town. He turned his horse and headed north.

—7—

In the small settlement a few miles northeast of Tahlequah known as Dog Town, George Tanner found the Barnes home without any difficulty. The cold drizzle was beginning to feel more and more like it would turn to sleet at any moment, but even so he hoped he'd be able to talk to Willit privately, outside. He dismounted, walked to the door of the small clapboard house, and knocked.

The door opened a crack, and a middle-aged woman with a drawn, hard face looked out at him suspiciously. George guessed that she might have been as much as half Cherokee.

"Mrs. Barnes?" he asked.

"What you want?"

"I'm George Tanner. I'm the deputy sheriff in Tahlequah. Is your son Willit at home?"

Before she could say anything more, the woman was shoved aside rudely and the door was pulled open a little wider. A man — a white man from his looks, George thought — maybe as old as sixty, stepped into the space and glared out at George. His eyes were rheumy, a watery blue, and his white hair looked as if it might have once been blond. He wore only a pair of baggy trousers over his long underwear, and they were held up by wide galluses. Among the other wrinkles on his face was a deep trench running from the right corner of his mouth down to his jawline. It was darkly stained from tobacco juice.

"What'd you call yourself?" he asked.

"Deputy Sheriff George Tanner. Are you Mr. Barnes?"

"I'm Barnes. What the hell's the law want here?"

"I'd like to talk with your son Willit, Mr. Barnes. Is he at home?"

"What do you want with my boy?" asked Barnes. "You going to arrest him?"

"No sir," said George. "I just want to talk to him. That's all."

"What's it all about?"

"Is he at home, Mr. Barnes? Could I see him?"

"I said what's it all about?"

George heaved a sigh. He decided that he would have to say at least a little more if he wanted to get past old man Barnes.

"Mr. Barnes," he said, "Willit threatened a man's life in Tahlequah yesterday in front of at least one witness. I believe that he said what he did in a moment of anger and likely did not mean it. I just want to talk to him and make sure that nothing more comes of it. That's all. Is he at home?"

"If he ain't under arrest," said Barnes,

"then you got no need to see him. Talk's talk. You get on out of here and leave us alone."

Barnes slammed the door in George's face, and George didn't waste any time trying again. He was getting cold standing out there anyway, and it was certain that old Barnes was not going to invite him in. He walked back to his horse, mounted up, and headed back toward Tahlequah.

"Mean old bastard," he muttered. The horse snorted as if in response.

Inside the house, still standing just inside the door, old man Barnes turned.

"Willit," he said, and his voice snapped out like a whip.

Willit Barnes, sitting in a chair at the table in the middle of the room, turned his head to face the old man.

"Yeah, Pa?"

"What the hell was that all about?"

"What, Pa?"

"Don't play dumb with me, boy. You heard."

"No sir," said Willit. "I didn't hear nothing. I mean, I heard you, but I couldn't hear whoever it was outside."

"No? Well, it was Tanner, Go-Ahead Rider's deputy. And he was looking for you. What you done to bring the law around here messing with us?"

"Me? I don't know, Pa. I ain't done nothing."

"You had yourself a fight yesterday, didn't you. You got your face all cut up. And then you wouldn't tell me nothing about it."

"Wasn't nothing to tell," said Willit.

Barnes took three long steps to the table, grabbed Willit by his shirtfront, and pulled him up out of his chair, knocking it over backward.

"Well, you'll tell me now," he said. "Tanner just said you threatened to kill a man. Is that true?"

"I don't know. I don't remember what I said. I might have said that. I was mad."

Barnes bent over and straightened the chair that had been knocked over a moment earlier, then pushed Willit back down into it. He reached for another chair, which he dragged out for himself. Then he sat directly in front of his son and stared him hard in the face.

"Now you'll tell me about that fight," he said. "Tell it all. First off, who was it with?"

"Lang," said Willit. "The schoolteacher. He's been seeing Hannah, and I told him to stop."

"He messed your face up pretty bad," said old Barnes. "What's *he* look like?"

Willit snorted. "I never even touched him," he said.

"What?"

"He's one of them fancy fighters. You know? Like a prizefighter. He held his dukes up like this, and he danced around and everything. I couldn't hit him for nothing."

The old man came up out of his chair suddenly, swinging his right arm and catching Willit across the side of the head with the back of his hand. Willit went sprawling on the floor.

"You let yourself get whipped by a god-damned school-teaching fancy-dancing Yankee dude? Get up, you whelp. I'll show you what a whipping really is."

Christopher Lang had gone to his office late Sunday evening. He had work that had to be done before his first Monday morning class, and he had spent most of his weekend visiting friends.

He remembered that when he had accepted the job, he had been more than a little apprehensive about going west to live among and teach the Indians. He had also been somewhat astonished at finding out that in his field, the classics, there was such a thing as a job teaching Indians. But the real revelation had come with the discovery that he would not be working for the government or for any Christian mission, but for the Indians themselves. His employer was the Cherokee Nation.

And he had settled into his new routine

easily and comfortably. He had made friends. He was becoming more and more familiar all the time with his surroundings, and he was even thinking about beginning a study of the Cherokee language.

So he did not begrudge himself his leisurely weekend, or resent having to work a little into the night on Sunday. He had arrived at his office shortly before sundown and had not worked long before he'd found it necessary to light a lamp on his desk. He decided that a couple of more hours, three at the most, would be sufficient to wrap things up for the night.

"It's dark enough," said Tommy Snail. "Why don't you go on and get it over with?"

Coley Fletcher was stretched out on the bed in the hotel room, staring up at the ceiling.

"Hell," he said, "I guess you're right."

He sat up on the edge of the bed and looked at Tommy.

"You going with me?" he asked.

"No," said Tommy. "I told you, I'm not having anything to do with this."

Coley stood up and got his coat. He pulled it on, then walked to the desk. After buttoning his coat about halfway up from the bottom, he grabbed the exam and tucked it inside the coat before he finished fastening it.

"I ain't asking you to do nothing," he said.

"I don't need you to actually go in the office with me or nothing like that. Hell, I don't want you to. I just thought you might go along with me. Keep me company. That's all. It's a long ways over there."

Tommy stood looking at the floor. He had spent the whole weekend with Coley, and Coley had used his money for their food and drink and for the hotel room. He felt guilty about the way in which he had spent the weekend. He felt guilty about being with Coley, considering the things Coley had done. But he also felt guilty that Coley had spent so much money on him. Money did not come easily in Tommy's family, and he reacted very keenly to the wasting of it.

"Besides," said Coley, "I never told you where I went a while ago, did I."

Tommy looked up at Coley.

"When I went out earlier this evening all by myself. I never told you, did I."

"No," said Tommy.

"I went down to the stable and rented a couple of saddle horses. We won't even have to walk. You can ride a horse, can't you?"

"Sure I can ride a horse."

"Well?"

There was a sharp rap at the window, and Lang jumped, startled. He put aside his Plutarch and turned his head to look, but he couldn't make out anything through the windowpane. There was another rap, and he stood up and walked to the window, raising it just a little.

"Mr. Lang," said a voice from the darkness.

Lang raised the window a little more and ducked to peek underneath. There stood Councilman Peck.

"Mr. Peck," said Lang, astonished, "what are you doing out there?"

"Go unlock the front door and let me in," said Peck. "I need to talk to you."

"Yes. Of course. Just a minute."

When Tommy and Coley rode up into the trees on the edge of the campus, the seminary building was dark again, all except the light in the window of old Broom. Coley dismounted and handed the reins of his horse to Tommy.

"Hold him for me," he said.

Tommy took the reins, feeling like an accessory to something or other, and Coley moved out to the edge of the trees. He stood there for a moment, looking around. The icy drizzle was still falling, and the night was much darker than it had been on Saturday.

That's good, thought Coley. I don't need to read nothing in there tonight anyhow. Just put it back where I got it from.

He started running toward the building, and about halfway across the lawn, he slipped, his feet shooting out in front of him.

With a curse, he came down hard on his back. He scrambled to his feet, looked around, then ran the rest of the way to the office window. It was open. Strange, he thought. He was sure he had closed it the night before.

Someone must have been in there since then, he thought. He hoped that it had not been Lang, or if it had been, that he had not looked in the desk drawer and noticed that the exam was missing. But why would Lang, or anyone else for that matter, open a window on a cold day — and then leave it open?

He reached up to shove the window open wider so that he could crawl through. Then he put his hands on the sill, heaved himself up, and scrambled into the office.

He straightened, and felt the pain in his back from the fall he had taken out on the yard. He took a couple of deep breaths, then started moving slowly and carefully. The soles of his boots were wet, and he didn't want to slip on the floor. Besides that, it was dark. He found his way around the desk, felt for the right drawer, and opened it. He pulled the exam out of his coat and dropped it in, then closed the drawer. As he started back around the desk, he stumbled over something and fell hard.

"Damn," he said.

He turned and looked. His eyes were beginning to adjust to the darkness, and when they focused on the thing he had tripped on, they opened wide in terror. His mouth gaped, and he made noises that sounded as if he could not make up his mind whether he wanted to say something or to scream. There was something there, something he had fallen over, but it was just a shape, a form. He couldn't quite make it out. He reached out to feel the shape, crawling toward it. As he put a hand on the floor, he felt it land in a pool of something wet and sticky.

"Oh!" he cried in spite of himself. He reached out farther and felt the shape, and he knew that it was the body of a man. He moved his face closer and squinted hard until the features before him began to take shape and he recognized them. Then he stood up, ran to the window, and jumped out as fast as he could. He ran the distance back to where Tommy waited with the horses, and he swung up quickly into the saddle.

"Come on," he said. "Let's get out of here."

"Did you put it back?" asked Tommy.

"Yes. Come on. Hurry it up."

"What's wrong, Coley?" asked Tommy.

"There's a dead man in there," said Coley. "It's Lang."

Tommy's first reaction to this startling announcement was that Coley was trying to frighten him. Coley was like that.

"Aw, come on, Coley," he said.

But Coley had already lashed his mount into a run.

"I ain't kidding," Coley shouted over his shoulder. "Let's get the hell out of here."

Still skeptical, but afraid that Coley might possibly be telling the truth, Tommy, his heart pounding, turned his horse and raced after his friend.

—8—

Tommy wanted some answers very badly, but Coley wouldn't slow down, much less talk. He lashed his rented horse like he was trying to win a race, and all Tommy could do was race after him all the way back into town. It seemed to Tommy like a much longer ride back in than it had been out, even though they were moving a lot faster. The cold rain was turning to sleet and it was stinging his face as they rode. At last they were back on Muskogee Avenue in front of the hotel, and they stopped. They tied the horses to the hitching rail in front and went inside and up the stairs to their room.

"Now tell me," said Tommy. "Will you tell me?"

"I done told you," said Coley, his face still white with fright. "There was a body in there on the floor. Laying facedown on the floor. I never even seen it, but I tripped over it and fell down. And then I felt it. I felt the blood, and I felt the body. Damn. I just walked right into him and tripped and fell on the floor."

"But you didn't see it?" said Tommy. "Maybe it wasn't really a dead man."

"It was a dead man, all right," said Coley. "There ain't no mistaking the way it felt when I touched it. And then I looked closer, and I seen it all right, and I seen who it was too."

"Are you sure it was Mr. Lang?"

"It was Lang. I got right in his face and looked. It was him."

"What did you do then?" asked Tommy.

"I got out of there as fast as I could," said Coley, "that's what I done. What the hell do you think? There was blood on the floor, and there was this body laying there. I —"

Coley suddenly remembered that he had put his hand in the blood. He hurried over to the water bowl and stuck his hand in it. With his other hand he scrubbed, but he could not see how much good he was doing. The boys had not bothered to light the lamp when they came in, and it was still dark in the room.

"We'd better go see the sheriff," said Tommy.

"No," said Coley.

"But we've got to tell someone."

"No we don't."

"Well, what're we going to do then?" asked Tommy.

"We ain't going to do nothing," said Coley. "You hear me? Nothing. We're going to school in the morning just like we always do. When the news gets out about Lang, we're going to be just as surprised as everyone else. No one seen us over there, and we don't know nothing. You hear? Nothing."

"But we can't just leave Mr. Lang lying on the floor in his office."

"He's dead," said Coley. "Nothing we do will make any difference to him one way or the other anymore. I'm sorry, Tommy. I know you liked him, but he's dead, and that's all there is to it."

But Tommy thought that there must be more to it. If there was really a body, as Coley said, if Mr. Lang was really lying in there dead on the floor, then what had happened to him? Had he been murdered? Coley had said there was blood. But who would want to kill Mr. Lang? And why?

Go-Ahead Rider knelt beside the body. It was a hell of a way to start a Monday morning. He had only just put the coffeepot on to boil, and George Tanner had just come in. Right behind George, Broom had come rushing in. He was excited, and he had talked to Rider in Cherokee. George had noticed the look that had come over Rider's face, and he had waited anxiously as Rider had put his hat and coat back on. Then Rider had said something to Broom, and Broom had left.

"What is it, Rider?" George had asked. "Is there a problem?"

"Yeah. There sure is. You'll want to come along, George," Rider had said, and then he had put a hand on George's shoulder. "Chris Lang has been murdered."

They had rushed on out to the Male Seminary and found Broom waiting for them at the front door. The old full-blood had pointed down the hallway and said something in Cherokee. Down the hall, J. P. Downing, the principal, stood waiting for them at the door to Lang's office.

They had hurried there to see it. The body was lying facedown between the desk and the door, with the head toward the desk. A knife protruded from the middle of the back, just below the shoulder blade. George, overcome with grief and anger, had turned ashen.

"George," Rider had said, "go on outside."

And George had stepped out into the hallway to lean against the wall. He stood there taking deep breaths and wondering who would do such a thing, and why. Downing stood in the doorway waiting as Rider studied the body and its surroundings.

Other than the knife, the most obvious thing to Rider was the handprint in the dried pool of blood right beside the body. The sheriff also took note of the upward angle of the knife, almost for sure the result of an underhand thrust. From the position of the body, Rider figured that Lang had been walking from the door to his desk when his killer struck from behind.

The window was opened on the far side of the room, and beneath the window the floor was messy. Someone had come in through the window with shoes wet and dirty from the damp lawn outside. The mess had been tracked from the window to the desk and on around to the body. There was no such mess between the body and the door.

"Mr. Downing," said Rider, "who discovered the body?"

"I did," said the principal. "I was in my office about fifteen minutes after eight when one of Mr. Lang's first-period students came in. He said that Mr. Lang had not showed up for class. Mr. Lang has never been late to class, and I thought that something might be wrong. I came down here to see if he was in his office, and — Well, this is what I found. I sent Broom after you immediately."

"Is everything here just exactly as you found it, Mr. Downing?" asked Rider. "Nothing been moved or —"

"Nothing has been touched," said Downing. "I guarded this door myself until your arrival."

Rider stood up and walked around the room, careful to avoid the tracks on the floor and the pool of blood. He noticed the lamp on the desk.

"Mr. Downing," he said, "did you turn off the lamp?"

"No sir. Like I told you, I didn't touch anything."

"There's still fuel in the lamp," said Rider, "so it didn't burn itself out. If this happened last night, he'd have had the lamp on. Could it have happened this morning, early? Did you notice anything unusual this morning?"

"No," said Downing. "Nothing. Except that the front door was unlocked when I arrived. I'm almost always the first one here, and so I unlock the door. I remember wondering who might have come in ahead of me this morning."

"Did Mr. Lang have a key to the outside door?"

"Yes. Of course. All faculty members do. They often come in to work in the evenings or on weekends."

"So Mr. Lang could have come in early this morning, before you arrived. He could have unlocked the building and come on down here to his office, and someone could have followed him in here."

"Sheriff," said Downing, "it was still dark when I arrived at the building this morning."

"So either Mr. Lang came in and sat in the dark," said Rider, "or his killer bothered to slow down and turn the lamp off before leaving."

Rider looked at Downing. He looked at the lamp on the desk, and he looked again at the mess on the floor beneath the window. Just then George stepped into the doorway.

"Excuse me," he said. Downing moved out of the way. "Do we have to leave Chris like that for much longer?"

"No, George," said Rider. "I think we can go ahead and have him moved now."

"I'll take care of it," said George.

"You don't have to, George," said Rider. "I can get —"

"No," said George. "It's okay. I want to do it. I think he'd have done as much for me."

"Mr. Downing," said Rider, turning his attention back to the principal, "you've got a bunch of boys here that need looking after. If I think of anything else I want to ask you, I'll come looking for you. Right now I think you can go on about your business."

Tommy Snail was sick in bed in the dormitory section of the second floor. When he had reported himself back at school that morning, Mr. Morrison, who was in charge of the rooms, had assumed that his illness was due to the weather. Perhaps it was, at least partly. Mostly, though, Tommy was sick with worry.

Neither he nor Coley had ever put the lamp on in the hotel room the night before, and with daylight, they had seen the blood on Coley's clothes. Apparently, Coley had wiped his hand on his clothes during the wild ride back to the hotel. He had not done a good job washing his hands in the cold water in the dark room, either. He was a mess.

"What're we going to do?" Tommy had asked. "You can't be seen like that."

"You go on out and bring the horses around to the back door," Coley had said. "Just do that for me, and that's all. I'll get out of town somehow. You go on back to school. Don't worry about me, and don't say nothing to nobody. You don't know nothing. Okay?"

"Are you sure?" said Tommy.

"You'll be all right. Don't worry."

"Okay."

But Tommy was worried. He felt bad about the untimely death of Mr. Lang, and he worried about who might have done it. And he was worried about Coley. He still thought that he should go to the sheriff, but Coley had told him not to, and he did not want to betray Coley. Besides, he realized with a twinge of horror, if the sheriff asked him, he could not say for sure that there really was a body. He only had Coley's word for that — and the bloodstains on Coley's clothes, of course. He had been outside with the horses some distance away.

Then he'd had another horrible thought. What if Mr. Lang had walked into the office and surprised Coley? What would Coley have done? Would he have killed to protect himself from detection? And what would Tommy be able to say about what had really happened in there? Nothing. He decided that Coley must be right. Just keep quiet.

Go-Ahead Rider was puzzled by several things he had seen in the office, but staring at them longer wouldn't do him any good. He stopped by the principal's office and asked Mr. Downing to lock the door to Lang's office and be sure that no one disturbed anything in there, then he went outside.

Pulling his coat tight around his body, he walked around the building to the open window. The ground was hard, with a layer of cold sleet on top of it, but it had been wet the night before. Below the window he saw several footprints, and they had been made by at least two different people. He could make out one boot mark and one shoe. The shoe marks seemed to lead back around to the front door, the way Rider had just come. But he couldn't be sure, since they faded out after a few paces.

But the boot marks were plainer, and they led across the campus toward a clump of trees. Rider reached up and shut the window. Then he followed the boot tracks and found where two horses had been in the trees. They had come in from the road and gone back out that way. There was no use in trying to see where they went from there. Two horses and two men, he thought. But then, the tracks indicated that only one man had gone from the horses to the window and back, and Rider couldn't be sure that man had been one of the riders. Two horses and maybe three men.

He walked back to the building, deliberately taking a fresh route. As he walked, he looked behind himself. On the sleet-hardened ground, he was not leaving a trail nearly as clear as the tracks he had been studying. He decided that those tracks had all been made the night before.

So two people, coming from two different directions, had been to Lang's window. Had they met there, purposely or otherwise, or had they come at different times? He realized that he had a couple more questions for Downing before he could leave and go back to the office.

George Tanner sat at his desk. He had made the necessary arrangements for the body, and laid out in front of him he had all of the items that had been discovered in the dead man's pockets. He also had the bloody knife. He had not yet been home to tell Lee the tragic news, nor had he bothered stopping by the Girty house to inform Hannah. He was still stunned by the news and by the actual sight. He was sad, for he had lost a friend, and he was angry, for someone had deliberately

94

taken the life of that friend.

He heard the outside door open, and he figured that it was probably Rider returning. But when the office door opened, it was Elwood Lovely who stepped inside.

"Howdy, George," said Lovely. "Damn, it's cold outside." He walked straight to the coffeepot and poured himself a cup. He took a sip. "Ah, that's good stuff. Good and hot. Rider around?"

"No."

"He sent me word that he's got a prisoner for me," said Lovely. "Name of Avery."

"Yes," said George.

"Well, if you'll fetch him out here for me," said the federal man, "I'll load him up in that wagon out there and haul him back to Muskogee."

"You might want to just leave him where he is for a while," said George.

"How come?" asked the deputy marshal.

"Rider's over at the Male Seminary," said George. "He'll be back soon, I expect. You'll want to talk to him. We went over there first thing this morning to investigate a murder. Christopher Lang. A teacher. A white man. It's your case, Mr. Lovely."

—9—

"Elwood," said Rider, "we've got a real puzzle out there at the school. I know that it's your problem, strictly speaking. Lang was a white man, and that puts the whole matter in your jurisdiction. But me and George, we'd sure like to help you out on this one, if you don't mind — unofficially, of course."

"I want to do everything I can to get the son of a bitch that killed Chris," added George Tanner. "He was a good friend. Officially, unofficially, I don't give a damn."

"Take it easy, George," said Rider.

"Well, boys," said Lovely, "I didn't make the laws, and I don't always understand them. Sometimes even when I do understand them, I don't agree with them. But none of that's my business anyhow. I've just got a job to do, and just between you and me, I welcome all the help I can get."

"Thank you, Elwood," said Rider. "We appreciate you; we really do. There've been some federal officers who've come here into the Cherokee Nation in the past that I'd just as soon shoot as have a cup of coffee with. You ain't one of them."

"I'm glad to hear that," said Lovely.

The three men were seated in Go-Ahead Rider's office in the National Prison — Rider behind his desk, George behind his, and Lovely in a straight-backed chair leaning against the wall to the far right of Rider's desk. Rider was smoking his pipe. All three men had cups in their hands, and all three cups were full of fresh, hot coffee.

Outside, the sun had emerged from behind the clouds, taking the worst of the chill out of the air and turning the previously frozen ground to mush. Rider was glad that he had investigated the footprints at the seminary early, while there was still a hard crust over everything.

"Well," said Lovely, "you want to start us off here by telling me what all you found out there? First off, tell me a little more about the victim. You say he was a schoolteacher?"

"Christopher Lang," said George. "He was originally from Connecticut. He had a degree in the classics from Hartford Seminary. Our council recruited him to teach Latin and Greek at the Male Seminary. He arrived down here at the beginning of the school year."

"That means he's been in town for about . . . four months," said Lovely. "Right?"

"Yeah," said George. "That's about right."

"Hardly long enough for a schoolteacher to make a bunch of enemies," said Lovely.

"It just takes one," said Rider.

"Yeah," said Lovely. "What else?"

"What else can you say about a man?" said George. "He was brilliant. He was doing a fine job with his students, as far as I could tell. He was liked by the students, the faculty, the administration. Everyone liked him."

"Not everyone," said Lovely.

"Well," said George, "everyone that I knew about. He adjusted pretty well to his new surroundings. Pretty quickly too. He just seemed to fit right in. And he was a good friend to me. It does seem like there ought to be more to say about a man after he's gone, doesn't it? I'm going to miss him a lot."

"He had one enemy that we know of," said Rider, "that we can put a name to."

"Willit Barnes," said George. "Chris was seeing a young Cherokee lady named Hannah Girty. Willit, it seems, thought that Hannah was his personal property, and he accosted them the other day while they were out for a walk. Chris gave him a sound beating, and Willit threatened to kill him."

"How'd you find out about that?" asked Lovely.

"We got the story from Lang and Hannah," said George.

"Do you think this Willit . . ."

"Barnes."

"Do you think this Willit Barnes is the one who done the killing?" asked Lovely.

98

"I don't know," said George. "I know who Willit is, but I can't say that I really know him. And men are apt to say just about anything in the middle of an argument or a fight."

"Right now," said Rider, "he's about all we've got, except for some kind of puzzling clues at the scene of the crime."

"Tell me about them," said Lovely. "How puzzling?"

"Well," said Rider, "the basics is clear enough." He picked up his cup and slurped some coffee, then put it down again. "From the way the body was found, it looks like Mr. Lang was walking from his office door toward his desk when someone stepped up behind him and stabbed him in the back. Underhand. Like so. He fell forward."

Rider puffed on his pipe, clouding up the air in the office.

"The puzzles?" asked Lovely.

"It seems like it must have happened sometime last night," said Rider. "Lang must have been working in his office. The window was standing open, and there was footprints outside that had to have been made last night. If someone had crawled through his window last night, and him not there, and he had come around later, he'd have shut the window."

"Stands to reason," said Lovely. "So he was killed last night."

99

"The lamp was turned off by someone after Lang was killed," Rider went on. "It was off when Mr. Downing found the body this morning, and it never burned itself out, because there was still plenty of fuel in it."

"Someone could have followed him in and killed him before he ever got the lamp lit," said Lovely.

"I don't think so," said Rider. "I think he was there for some time, because I think he had at least two visitors while he was working in the office."

"Two?"

"There was two different sets of footprints outside the window. One man was wearing boots. The other'n was wearing shoes. They didn't come together, and they didn't leave together. I suppose they could've met there and then gone separate ways, but I kind of doubt it."

"So someone crawled through the window and killed him?"

"Someone crawled through the window for sure," said Rider. "There was muddy prints on the office floor below the window, and they tracked on around behind the desk and over to where the body was laying. Then they went back to the window. And there was a handprint in the blood on the floor. But I ain't sure that the one who made them prints is the one who killed him. Oh yeah — the boot prints outside came from and went back to a clump of trees where two horses had been waiting."

"Two horses?" said Lovely. "Two men."

"Likely," said Rider.

Elwood Lovely dropped the front legs of his chair to the floor, got up, and walked over to the stove. He refilled his coffee cup, then turned to face Rider.

"I don't get it," he said. "You got evidence that someone crawled through the window, and you got his tracks going to the body, yet you ain't sure he did it?"

Rider looked around the room a moment, then stood.

"Get up, George," he said. He walked over to George's desk and shoved it around at a different angle. He looked from the desk to the window and then the door. Then he pointed at the window.

"Say we're in Mr. Lang's office," he said. "There's the window. There's the desk, and there's the door. Move over there, Elwood. Yeah. Right there. Now take about one step toward the desk."

He positioned Lovely about halfway between the door and George's desk.

"You're walking toward your desk," he said, then he himself walked over to the window. "You're walking to your desk, and I just climbed through the window. We're looking each other right in the face."

"Yeah?" said Lovely.

"You think I can walk around behind you and stab you in the back?"

"Not likely," said the deputy.

"That's what I said." Rider moved George's desk back where it had been. "Now that other set of prints, that's even more interesting to me."

"The shoes?" said George.

"Yeah. They come right up to the window, and then they go around the corner of the building, like they're headed for the front door."

"That's the second visitor?" asked Lovely.

"Well, it's the other one," said Rider. He walked back behind his desk and sat down again. "I don't know which one was first and which was second."

"But if he could get in the door," said George, "why'd he go around to the window in the first place?"

"Because he couldn't get in the door. Mr. Downing told me that when a teacher goes into the building to work in the evenings or on weekends or such, he has instructions to lock the front door behind him. So Lang, if he done like he was told, unlocked the front door, stepped inside, locked it again, and then walked down the hall to his office. The man in the shoes didn't go to the window to crawl through or to just spy or to say hello. He went to the window to get Lang's attention and ask him to open the door. George, you've got all that stuff from Lang's pockets."

"Yeah," said George. "It's all right here on my desk."

"Notice anything peculiar?"

Lovely walked over to look at the items with George.

"Well, no," said George.

"It looks pretty ordinary to me," said Lovely. "A bit of pocket change, a penknife, wallet —"

"What don't you see there?" asked Rider.

"Well, I don't know," said George. "I —"

"Aw, come on, Rider," said Lovely. "What the hell are you getting at?"

"No keys. They ain't in the office either."

"No keys?" said George. "You're right."

"He had to have his keys to get in," said Lovely, "and to let that other fellow in."

"The man in the shoes," said Rider. "He got Lang's attention at the window, then walked around to meet him at the door. Lang unlocked the door and let him in. Then he likely locked the door again. The man followed him to the office —"

"And stabbed him in the back as they were going in," said George.

"Likely," said Rider. "Then to get out again, he had to take Lang's keys, but before he left, he put out the light."

"We got him," said George, excited. Then he drooped back in his chair again. "But who the hell is he?"

"How clear was them footprints?" asked Lovely.

"I could tell they was shoes," said Rider. "Too big for me. That's about all."

"That ain't much," said Lovely.

"No," Rider agreed. "It ain't, so we're right back where we started."

"Where's that?" said George.

"Back to Willit Barnes."

They heard the outside door creak open, then bang shut again, and they looked at the office door, waiting to see who would walk through. Then the door was pushed open, and a wiry, middle-aged man in dirty work clothes stepped in.

"Rider," he said. "George. Oh, Mr. Lovely. I didn't expect to see you here."

" 'Siyo, Curly," said Rider, greeting him in Cherokee. "What can we do for you?"

"Well, it's the damnedest thing," said Curly. "Yesterday evening, old Coyne Fletcher's boy come by my barn."

"Coley?" said Rider.

"Yeah. That's his name. Anyhow, he said that he was staying in town over the weekend. I thought them boys was supposed to stay at the school unless they was going home, but then that ain't none of my business. He said he wanted to rent a couple of riding horses, and he paid me up front, so I let him have the horses. He said he'd have them back first thing Monday. That's today.

He never brought them.

"Well, I figured that if he was staying in town, he'd have to be at a hotel or a boardinghouse, so I went out looking around, and down behind the National Hotel, I found one of my horses."

"Just one?" said Rider.

"Just one. I went inside and asked for him, and they said that he'd been there, all right, him and another boy, but they was gone."

"Okay, Curly," said Rider. "We'll check into it for you.

"I appreciate it, Rider," said Curly. "That's a good horse. I need him back. 'Course, that ain't all I'm worried about. I don't think the Fletcher kid would steal a horse; hell, his daddy's rich. Something might've happened to the boy. Anyhow, I figured you'd ought to know about it. You'll let me know when you find out anything?"

"Sure will, Curly," said Rider. "Thanks for coming in."

Curly left the office, and Rider looked at George.

"Two horses," said George.

"Coley Fletcher was running with Tommy Snail this weekend," said Rider. "They was both in Lang's class, too."

"Two leads," said George.

"Yeah." Rider stood up, grabbed his two Colts, and tucked them into his waistband. "George," he said, "why don't you follow up

105

this new lead. See what you can find out about Coley Fletcher."

"Yes sir."

George got his hat and coat and left the office.

"Elwood," said Rider, "I sure don't want to tell you how to proceed . . ."

"Tell me, Rider," said Lovely. "I ain't proud."

"All right then. Let's you and me get in your wagon and drive over to Dog Town."

"Dog Town?"

"That's where Willit Barnes lives."

—10—

George rode to the front of the National Hotel, dismounted, hitched his mount to the rail, and stepped up onto the sidewalk. He went inside the lobby and found Sim Potter, a nervous young man, behind the counter.

"Hello, Sim," he said.

"Deputy," said Sim, flinching. "I knew it. I am not surprised to see you here at all. No sir. I was afraid of something like this."

"Like what?" asked George.

"Well, you've come about Coley Fletcher, ain't you?"

"Yes, I have, but how did you know that?"

"The stolen horse, of course," said Sim. "I guess you wouldn't care about the mess he left me upstairs, but I figured you'd be around because of the horse. You or Mr. Rider. Oh yes. And the whiskey. I just knew there was going to be some trouble."

George leaned his elbows on the counter and looked Sim in the face.

"All right, Sim," he said. "Slow down. Curly came to see us about his horse, so I know about that, but what's all the rest of this about?"

"Well, after Curly came in asking for

Coley, saying that his horse was gone, I went up to check the room. Coley had rented a room for the whole weekend, you know. Paid for it in advance. I knocked on the door and didn't get no answer, so I used my key and went in. Well, they was gone, all right. And the room was a mess."

"They?"

"Well, yes. Coley had another fellow with him. That's why he had rented two horses, I suppose, but Coley was the only one who signed the register. I don't know who the other one was."

"Did you see him?"

"Well, yes, I saw him. They came in and out several times. You know, I don't like to get anyone in trouble, but they did leave me a mess. They had been drinking too; I know they had. I mean, I never seen them at it, but there was a whiskey bottle in the room too. Empty."

"Full-blood boy?" asked George.

"What?"

"The other boy. Was he a full-blood?"

"Oh. Yeah. I'd say. He had the look, you know?"

"Go on, Sim."

"Go on what?"

"The room was a mess."

"Oh. Yeah. Well, I went on in, and the first thing I noticed was that the bedclothes was all gone. Stole. They stole my sheets and blankets and pillowcases. That's what they done. Oh yes, and my towel too. It's gone. Now why would they do a thing like that? I'm going to have to write a letter to Mr. Coyne Fletcher and tell him about this and ask him to pay for the stole items."

"Is that all?" asked George.

"Ain't that enough?" said Sim. "But it ain't all. No sir. There was that whiskey bottle, like I said. Did I say that? Anyway, there was that whiskey bottle. That's against the law. I could get in trouble for that. Mr. Tanner, I swear to you, I don't know where they got it, and I do not approve of whiskey being drunk in the rooms of my hotel."

"Don't worry about that," said George. "No one's blaming you for anything. Go on."

"Well, that's about it, I guess, except the floor's all muddy. A real mess."

"Sim," said George, "has the room been cleaned yet?"

"Well, no. I been awful busy today, and we're shorthanded —"

"Take me up there and let me in the room," said George.

Sim led the way and unlocked the door. George took his key, sent him on back to work, and stepped inside the room alone. He looked at the bed, stripped of its covers, like Sim had said. He turned toward the small table with the jug and bowl. There was no towel. The bowl had been emptied, its contents probably tossed out the window, George thought. He picked it up and examined it closely. It was streaked a little, like someone had tried to wipe it clean with a cloth. George rubbed the streaks with his fingers and looked closely at his fingertips. Blood? Could it be? He looked toward the desk and saw the whiskey bottle. Then he noticed the papers.

He stepped over to the desk for a closer look. There was a pen, used and left dirty, an uncapped ink bottle, and several sheets of blank paper.

He locked the door when he left and stopped back by the desk to instruct Sim to be sure that no one cleaned the room or removed anything from it until further word from the sheriff's office. Then he went out back where Curly had discovered his one horse. He looked up and down the alley and saw nothing unusual, but as he turned to go back inside, he noticed a rumpled sheet of paper on the ground. He picked it up and was astonished to see that the writing — clumsy, awkward, messy — was in Latin. He read a few lines. It's an exam, he said to himself, an exam on Plutarch.

Elwood Lovely hauled back on the reins, bringing the wagon to a stop in front of the Barnes home in Dog Town. He set the brake, and he and Go-Ahead Rider climbed down out of the wagon. The ground was muddy all around. There was no way to avoid it, so they slogged their way up to the front door. They were only a couple of paces away when the door was opened from inside, and there stood old man Barnes, a shotgun in his hands.

"I told that other lawman to stay away from us," he said, "and I meant it. Ain't nobody here done nothing that's any of your business."

"Mr. Barnes," said Lovely, "I would advise you to put down that gun."

"Mr. Lovely here is a deputy United States marshal, Mr. Barnes. We just want to have a talk with Willit," said Rider. "Ain't no call for trouble here."

"I done had a talk with Willit," said Barnes. "You want to put him in jail for getting himself whipped by a Yankee schoolteacher?"

"Mr. Barnes," said Lovely, "your son threatened to kill Mr. Lang —"

"Words. That's all that is. Words."

"Mr. Lang was killed last night," said Lovely. "Stabbed in the back. We'd like to talk to your son."

Barnes lowered the shotgun a bit, and his jaw dropped along with it.

"The schoolteacher's been killed?" he said.

"That's right. Now are you going to let us in? Because if you don't, we'll be back before the day is over with a whole posse, and there will be federal charges filed against both you and your son."

"Put down the gun and let us in," said Rider. "We didn't come here to arrest Willit. We just want to talk to him. That's all."

Barnes let the gun drop down to his left side. He stepped back, leaving the door opened wide.

"Come on then," he said. "Get it over with so you can get out of here and leave us in peace."

As he followed Lovely into the dark hovel, Rider thought that if he had to describe the place later, he wouldn't know how. It seemed to him like piles of rags, some on the floor, some on boxes, some on pieces of old furniture. Rags also dangled from the walls and from the ceiling. Some might have been clothes; others might have been serving as curtains.

Barnes made a wild gesture with his right arm toward a back corner of the room.

"Well, go on," he said. "There he is. Ask your questions and be done."

Rider squinted toward the corner, past the woman who stood by the table looking like not much more than a rag herself, to a pile of something that formed a sort of bed. There, lying on the heap, or in it, only his head and one arm and shoulder exposed to view, was Willit Barnes. The two lawmen walked across the room.

"Elwood," said Rider, "this is Willit Barnes.

Willit, this here is Elwood Lovely. He's the deputy United States marshal from Muskogee. We got a few questions we'd like to ask you."

Willit did not answer. He looked from Rider to Lovely, and then Rider noticed the puffy face. He leaned forward for a closer look. One eye was swollen shut, and Willit's lips were badly cut and bruised. There was dried blood on the side of his head and on his mouth. The exposed arm and shoulder also showed bruises.

"Willit," said Rider, "are you okay?"

"I'm okay," Willit muttered through his swollen and scabbed-over lips.

"Did Chris Lang do all that to you?"

"He done some of it," said Willit. "A little."

"I done it," roared old man Barnes from behind Rider and Lovely. "I thrashed him for getting himself whipped by a schoolteacher and for bringing the law out here to bother us."

Lovely turned toward Barnes, an unbelieving look on his face.

"You did that to your own son?" he asked.

"I believe in raising them right," said Barnes. "When they misbehave, whip them. That's the only way they learn. If everyone done it, we wouldn't have no criminals. It's in the Bible — or don't you read the Bible?"

"Mr. Barnes," said Rider, "if you don't

mind, we'd like to talk to Willit alone."

"He ain't fit to get up," said Barnes, "and I ain't going to be put out of my own home."

"Shadrach," the woman said, the suddenness of her unexpected voice startling everyone in the room, "let's you and me go out and fetch us in some fresh water."

Without saying a word, Barnes propped his shotgun in a corner of the room, picked up a bucket, and followed his wife outside.

"Willit," said Rider, "did you have a fight with Chris Lang on Saturday?"

"Well, yeah. I did."

"What was it all about?"

"I told him to leave Hannah alone," said Willit, "and he wouldn't listen."

"So you fought with him?"

"Yeah."

"And he got the best of you," said Lovely.

Willit looked downward with his swollen eyes.

"Yeah. I reckon he whipped me."

"Did you threaten to kill him?" asked Rider.

"I guess I did," said Willit. "I don't know. Probably I said it. I was mad; I don't know what I said. But if I said it, I didn't mean it. Not really. I ain't never killed anyone."

"Do you own a knife?" asked Lovely.

"Huh?"

"Do you own a knife?"

"Well, yeah. Sure. Don't everyone?"

"Where is it right now?"

"Well, I don't know. Over there on that shelf, I guess." He tried to turn and point, but he fell back onto his rag heap with a groan. "What you want to know that for?"

Rider stepped over to the shelf. It was about chin-high on the wall and covered with rags. He looked closely and found a hunting knife in a sheath. He picked it up and showed it to Lovely. Then he replaced it.

"Do you carry that knife with you?" asked Lovely.

"No," said Willit. "Only when I'm hunting is all."

"Do you own another knife?"

"No. What's this all about anyway?"

"Willit," said Rider, "when did this happen to you?"

"What?"

"When did your — your pa beat you up?"

Willit tried again to duck his head in shame, but all he could do was lower his eyelids.

"It was just after Mr. Tanner left here," he said. "Why?"

"Willit, Mr. Lang was stabbed to death in his office last night," Rider said. "You had a fight, and you threatened to kill him. We had to come out and talk to you because of that, but I don't think we'll be bothering you again."

"Someone killed him?"

Rider nodded.

"Do you know of anyone else who might have had a grudge against Mr. Lang?" he asked.

"No," said Willit. "No. I didn't hardly know him, really. I wanted him to leave Hannah alone, but I never wanted him to get killed. I guess I did say that, but I never . . . I'm sorry he got killed. I really am. You know, he was one hell of a fistfighter."

"All right," said Rider. "Thank you." He turned toward Lovely. "Let's go," he said. They walked across the room, and Lovely pulled the door open and went out. Rider was about to step outside, then hesitated. Turning back toward Willit, he said, "You have a job, don't you?"

"Yeah."

"If I was you, I'd try to save up enough to move out of here just as soon as I was healthy enough to do it."

They slogged through the mud and climbed back up into the wagon, and old man Barnes appeared from behind the house.

"Are you done here?" he asked.

"Yeah, we're done," said Rider.

"Mr. Barnes," said Lovely, "I'd arrest you if I thought I could make a charge stick. I'd dearly love locking you away."

"For what?" said Barnes.

"For damn near beating that boy to death. If you'll take my advice, you won't ever do that again."

He flicked the reins angrily, and the wagon gave a lurch and pulled out onto the road. He drove along for a space in silence. Finally he spoke.

"Rider," he said, "I don't know Willit Barnes. I don't know if he deserves whipping or not, but it burns my ass to see a man beat his own son like that."

"One thing's for sure," said Rider.

"What's that?"

"Willit didn't kill Chris Lang. The old man beat him up before the killing took place, and poor old Willit can't get up, much less get himself over to the seminary to kill someone."

"Yeah, I guess you're right about that," said Lovely. He pulled the reins to turn the team. "We crossed one suspect off our list."

"Yeah," said Rider.

"But we've got another one."

"We do?" said Rider.

"Yep. That old bastard Shadrach," said Lovely. "Shadrach Barnes. He sure seemed to be insulted that a schoolteacher whipped his boy."

—11—

On his way to the school from the hotel, George stopped by the home of Hannah Girty and her mother. It was only a short distance out of the way, and George didn't think that anyone had bothered to speak to Hannah about the recent unfortunate events. She had seemed close to Chris, George thought. Besides, it was just possible that she might be able to help in some way.

Inside the Girty home, George sat uncomfortably stiff. Hannah was red-eyed and sad. George wondered just how serious the situation between her and Chris Lang had gotten.

"Hannah," he said, "I can't tell you how sorry I am about this. You know, Chris was my very good friend. I promise you that we'll find out what happened — who's responsible."

"I know, George," said Hannah. "Chris talked about you a lot. He sure did like you."

"Hannah," said George, "do you think that Willit Barnes could have had anything to do with it?"

"Willit?" she said, incredulous. "You mean because of the fight?"

"Yes."

"Oh, no," she said. "I couldn't believe that of Willit. He was mad, and he might have tried to fight Chris again, but he wouldn't ever do . . . what was done."

"That's what I think too, Hannah," said George, "but I had to ask you. Is there anyone else you can think of who might have had some reason to want Chris dead?"

"No. I'm sorry, George, but I can't think of a soul. Chris was so good. Why would anyone want to do that to him?"

She started to cry, and George stood up, still feeling awkward.

"Well," he said, "if anything occurs to you, please let me know. I'm sorry I had to bother you with this, Hannah."

He excused himself and got out of the house. Mounted again and on his way to the seminary, he thought, I hope I never have to go through anything like that again.

Coley Fletcher rode hard until he was several miles north of Tahlequah. Then the worst of his panic began to subside, and he realized that he would likely kill the horse if he didn't slow down. Besides, he had another problem to deal with. He hauled back on the reins, slowing the pace of the laboring beast beneath him, then turned it east toward the riverbank. He rode slowly, studying the rocks and brush along the edge of the water.

At last he spied a likely spot, and he

119

stopped the horse. Taking with him the muddy and bloodstained bundle he carried, he walked to a cluster of small boulders not far from the water's edge. He put down the bundle and, using both hands, rolled aside one of the rocks. Then he tucked the bundle in where the rock had been and rolled the rock back into place.

He sat back and breathed deeply for a moment, then crawled to the water and dipped his hands in. The water was sharp with cold. He raised his cupped hands to his face and splashed it with the cold water. He felt momentarily stunned, but also refreshed. He stood, walked back to the horse, and swung back up into the saddle. Once again, he turned the animal's head to the north and rode on.

George Tanner walked into the principal's office at the seminary.

"Mr. Downing," he said.

The harried principal looked up from his work.

"Oh, Mr. Tanner," he said. "What can I do for you?"

"I'm sorry to have to bother you again, Mr. Downing," said George.

"Oh no. Please. Anything I can do to help. This is a terrible business. Terrible. I was just working on our schedule. Mr. Lang's classes, you know. It seems awfully cold to have to worry about such things at a time like this, but something has to be done. All those students."

"Of course," said George. "I understand. I'll try not to take too much of your time. I'm looking for two students: Coley Fletcher and Tommy Snail. Are they here today?"

"I — I don't know. I've been in such a muddle here today. Uh, come with me, please. Mr. Morrison is on dormitory duty today. He'll have checked the roll."

George followed Downing out of the office and down the corridor. At the far end of the hall the principal knocked on a closed door. A voice from the other side responded.

"Yes?" it said. "Come in, please."

The principal opened the door and leaned in.

"Mr. Morrison?" he said.

"Yes sir?"

"Mr. Morrison, do you know Mr. Tanner, our deputy sheriff?"

Morrison stood up from behind his small desk and stepped toward the door. Downing stepped aside, and Morrison and George shook hands. George thought that the teacher's hand seemed clammy.

"We've never actually met," said Morrison. "How do you do?"

"Mr. Tanner has some questions about two of our students," said Downing. "I told him that you could help him."

"I'll do my best," said Morrison.

"If you'll excuse me," said Downing, "I'll get back to work."

"Thank you, Mr. Downing," said George as the principal headed down the hallway toward his office. George turned back to face Morrison, a young man with soft, smooth skin. He was immaculately dressed, and he smelled of strong lilac water. His oiled hair was blond and prematurely thin on top.

"How may I help you, Mr. Tanner?" Morrison asked.

"I'm looking for Coley Fletcher and Tommy Snail," said George.

Morrison's face took on a sudden worried look.

"Are they in some sort of trouble?" he asked. "Nothing to do with this terrible business about Mr. Lang, I hope."

"I just want to talk to the boys," said George. "Are they here?"

"Well, Coley didn't show up at all this morning," said Morrison, "but Tommy is here. The poor thing is upstairs in bed, though. He has a fever. I think he developed a bad cold out in the rain yesterday."

"I'd like to see him," said George.

"Yes, of course. Please follow me."

Elwood Lovely realized that the case of the murdered seminary teacher might occupy quite some time, so he sent a message to his office in Muskogee explaining the situation, then went to the National Hotel to get himself a room. He had just registered with Sim and dropped his room key into a vest pocket and turned to leave when a big man stood up from one of the lounge chairs and stepped toward him, his hand out.

"Excuse me," said the man. "I didn't mean to eavesdrop, but did I understand you to say that you're a deputy United States marshal?"

"I am. Elwood Lovely from the Muskogee office."

The two men shook hands.

"I'm Forbes Winters. Pleased to make your acquaintance, Mr. Lovely. Eh, could I have a few moments of your time?"

"What's on your mind?" Lovely asked.

"I represent the railroad interests," said Winters. "You might say we have the same goals, you and me. I mean, what's good for the railroad is good for the country, right? Progress. It occurred to me that you might have some insights into these people down here that could help me. We could get together up in my room. Let me buy you a drink of good brandy, and we could have a leisurely conversation regarding the future of the railroad in the Cherokee Nation."

"Mr. Winters," said Lovely, "I —"

He stopped and considered what he had been about to say — that he had no interest in politics; that he was well aware of the current conflict between the railroad and the Cherokee

Nation; that of course he knew that the United States government, his employer, was on the side of the railroad but that even so, it was not his job to interfere in the matter, and in fact, if the truth were known, his own personal sympathies regarding the railroad issue were secretly on the side of the Cherokees. That was what he had been about to say, or something along those lines. But he changed his mind.

"Sure, Mr. Winters," he said. "Why not? Right now?"

"There's no time like the present," said Winters, a broad smile spreading across his round, red face. He led the way up to his room and unlocked the door. Then he stepped aside and with a grand sweep of his arm, invited Lovely to go in.

"Take a chair, Mr. Lovely," he said, following the deputy into the room and shutting the door. Lovely found a straight chair and placed it a couple of feet away from the wall. He sat down and shoved the chair off its two front legs, leaning its back against the wall.

"Are you comfortable there?" asked Winters.

"Just fine," said Lovely.

Winters opened a leather satchel and brought out a bottle of brandy, holding it up to show the label to Lovely. He put it on the table, produced two stemmed glasses from the same satchel, and poured a goodly amount of brandy into each. Taking a glass in each hand, he stepped over to Lovely and handed him one. Lovely took the snifter in his left hand. Winters raised his own high over his head.

"Here's to the future," he said.

Lovely lifted his glass and watched as Winters sipped the brandy. Then Lovely let the front legs of his chair drop to the floor. He stood up and walked over to the fancy satchel and poured the contents of his snifter into it.

"Hey. What's the meaning of this?" Winters spluttered. "What do you think you're doing?"

"*Your* immediate future's in the jailhouse," said Lovely. He picked up the brandy bottle and dropped it back into the satchel, not bothering to recap it.

"Now see here," said Winters.

"Don't you know that it's against the law to introduce liquor into the Indian Territory, Mr. Winters?" Lovely asked.

"Oh, come on," said Winters. "That's for the Indians. We both know that."

"The law makes no distinctions, Mr. Winters."

Lovely reached out and took the glass from Winters's hand and dropped it into the satchel. Then he picked up the satchel in his own left hand.

"Let's go," he said.

"Do you actually mean to arrest me?" blustered Winters.

"You're under arrest, Mr. Winters," said Lovely, "for possession of alcoholic spirits within the boundaries of the Indian Territory. Is that clear enough for you? Now let's go."

"You can't do this to me," Winters shouted. "I'll have your job for this."

Lovely pulled out his revolver in his right hand, leveled it at Winter's ample belly, and thumbed back the hammer. Winters's face paled.

"You might," said Lovely, "but you'll set a spell in the jailhouse first. Get going. I ain't going to tell you again."

Tommy Snail started to tremble when he saw George Tanner, in the company of Mr. Morrison, walking toward his bed. They know, he thought. They know. I told Coley we'd never get away with it. I told him. And it's not just cheating anymore.

The news of the brutal slaying of Christopher Lang had spread like wildfire all around the school by this time, and as the deputy sheriff approached Tommy, the image of Coley Fletcher in his bloody coat returned vividly to the nervous boy's consciousness. He wondered again if Coley had told him everything.

Morrison stopped at the head of the bed, George at the foot. Morrison sat down on a chair and leaned over Tommy. He put a gentle hand on Tommy's forehead and spoke in a soothing voice.

"Tommy, how are you feeling?"

"Not so good," Tommy said, and George

could see the boy tense up at the touch of the teacher.

"Do you know Mr. Tanner, the deputy sheriff?"

"Yes sir."

"Do you feel up to talking with Mr. Tanner for a few minutes? He'd like to ask you some questions."

"I guess so," said Tommy.

"I'd like to talk to him alone," said George.

Morrison looked up abruptly at George. He seemed both annoyed and disappointed.

"Oh," he said. "Of course. Excuse me." He got up and left the room. George moved to the chair and sat down.

"You stay out in that cold drizzle too long, Tommy?" he asked.

"I guess."

"You were with Coley Fletcher this weekend, weren't you."

"Yes sir."

"Coley rented a room over in the National Hotel."

"Yes."

"What did you two boys do with yourselves all weekend?"

"Oh, nothing much," said Tommy. "We just messed around."

"You drink a little whiskey, did you?"

Tommy lowered his eyes. He didn't answer.

"Tommy," said George, "I've been to the room. It hasn't been cleaned since you left.

There's a whiskey bottle on the desk."

"I didn't drink much of it. I didn't like it. Are you going to put me in jail for drinking whiskey?"

"No, I don't think so. That's not what I'm really interested in right now anyway, although Sheriff Rider might want to ask you later on where you got it."

"I don't know," said Tommy. "Coley got it somewhere. I wasn't with him when he got it."

George reached into his pocket and pulled out the rumpled paper with the Latin written on it. He smoothed it as much as he could and handed it to Tommy.

"Can you tell me anything about this?" he asked.

Tommy's heart was pounding in his chest. He held the hateful paper in front of his eyes for only a brief moment. It was the source of all the problems.

"Have you ever seen that before, Tommy?" asked George.

"Yes sir. Not close. I didn't want to look at it. I told Coley not to do it. I even offered to study with him, but he wouldn't listen to me. I don't cheat. I never cheated, and I didn't look at that exam either."

"How did Coley get that exam?" George asked, but he knew the answer already.

"He climbed through the window to Mr. Lang's office," said Tommy.

"When was this?"

"Saturday night."

"Saturday? Are you sure?"

"Yes sir."

"Don't lie to me, Tommy."

"I'm not. It was Saturday. He took it back to the hotel to copy it, and he was supposed to return it, but he fell asleep. He'd been drinking all that whiskey. So . . ."

"So? Go on."

"So he had to wait until Sunday night, until it got dark again, and then he took it back."

"And you went with him, didn't you. He rented two horses, and the two of you rode out here together."

"Yes sir."

"All right, Tommy," said George. "Calm down. I'm not out to get you. I just want some answers. When you came out here Sunday night, did you see anyone else around?"

"No sir."

"Was there anyone inside the office?"

Tommy thought about what Coley had told him. Just keep quiet. Don't tell anyone anything. But Coley had run away. Coley didn't have to face the lawman, and Coley didn't know that they already seemed to know everything anyway.

"I didn't go in," said Tommy. "I waited with the horses. But when Coley came out, he acted real scared. I'd never seen Coley act scared before, and he said that there was a dead man in the office. It was Mr. Lang.

Coley said it was too dark to see. He said he tripped over — over the body. He didn't see it at first. He — he felt it."

"Did he get blood on his hands?" George asked. "Is that why he took the sheets and the towel?"

"He had it all over his clothes, too," said Tommy. "I think that's why he didn't come back to school — he didn't have any clothes to change into, and he didn't want to go out around town like that. He ran off, and I came back to school. I knew you'd find out. I knew it. I told Coley that we should go tell the sheriff, but he said not to."

"All right, Tommy," said George. "I know it's not going to be easy, but you just try to relax. Get some rest and get well. We'll get this thing sorted out." He stood up, ready to leave.

"You're not going to arrest me?"

"I don't think so, Tommy."

"Are you going to tell Mr. Downing what I did?"

"No. But maybe *you* ought to think about telling him."

George waited, but Tommy made no response.

"Well," George said, "I might be back to ask you some more questions, or Sheriff Rider or Deputy Marshal Lovely might. Oh. Do you know where Coley went?"

"No sir," said Tommy. "All I know is that he ran off."

—12—

Rider was out of the office when Lovely marched Winters in, so Lovely, familiar with Rider's jail, helped himself to the keys and locked the railroad man into the cell next to the one which held his other prisoner, Bob Avery.

"This is an outrage," said Winters as Lovely locked the door. "I'm warning you, Deputy, you'll regret this. You'll be sorry you ever met me."

"Hell, Winters," said Lovely, "I'm already sorry I met you. You're a disgrace to our race."

"This is an outrage, I tell you," Winters shouted.

"It sure as hell is," said Avery. "I want out of this goddamned Indian jail. You got no right to keep me in here."

"Avery," said Lovely, "have you ever been throwed in the federal jail over in Muskogee?"

"No. I ain't. I ain't no common criminal."

"Well, when I put you in over there, you'll wish you were back here. This place is a whole lot nicer. Enjoy it while you can, gunfighter."

He walked down the hall and disappeared,

with Avery shouting after him.

"You son of a bitch. You dirty bastard. I'll get you for this. You'll be sorry. If I have to wait a hundred years, I'll get you."

Winters listened with interest to Avery's diatribe. He waited until Avery's rage had calmed, then walked over to the bars that separated the two cells.

"Excuse me, sir," he said.

Avery turned and looked at Winters, a hard scowl on his face.

"What do you want?" he said.

"I take it that you're a white man and a prisoner of this deputy marshal."

"Yeah? Well, you take it right. Who the hell are you?"

"My name is Forbes Winters. I represent some major railroad interests. I too ran afoul of Mr. Lovely."

"Oh yeah?" said Avery. "What'd you do?"

"I offered the officer a drink of brandy, and he arrested me for possessing alcohol in the Indian Territory."

Avery guffawed, and Winters puffed up and turned red.

"I intend to have my revenge," said Winters when Avery had quieted down some. "I have influential friends in high places. At the very least, I'll have his job. In the meantime, my friend, if you can come up with a way to get us out of here, I can be very grateful."

"You mean . . ."

"I mean I can be very generous."

Avery turned his back on Winters and walked across to the other side of his cell. He stared away in silence for a moment. Then he turned back around. He studied Winters with a sideways look for a short while.

"Ah, you're full of shit," he said. "Suppose I could bust you loose. Where would you go, a man like you, with U.S. marshals on his ass with a whiskey warrant, and a jailbreaking charge to boot?"

"If you could just get me out of here and to the nearest railroad, I would go straight to the federal marshal's office in Washington, D.C., and get the warrant dismissed and Mr. Lovely fired. I could also get the charges against you dismissed, my friend, whatever they might be."

Avery paced away, then turned around and looked again at Winters. He looked at the expensive clothes and took note of the man's arrogant posture.

"Can you really do that?" he asked.

"I can do that and more."

"When you said you could be real generous, just exactly what did you mean by that?"

Rider walked into the office and tossed some papers on his desk. Lovely was sitting in the chair against the wall.

"Howdy, Sheriff," said Lovely. "I just took advantage of your hospitality again. Hope you don't mind."

"How's that?" asked Rider, moving around behind his desk to settle in his chair.

"I arrested a damn pompous railroad man for possession of spirits, and I locked him in one of your cells. I'll take him along with me back to Muskogee whenever I take Avery. Okay?"

"Yeah," said Rider. "It's okay with me, but are you sure you want to be messing with them railroad men? They got friends and allies in the government. They might could hurt you, Elwood."

"Oh, I know it, but the son of a bitch just pissed me off, Rider. Hell, I was looking for a job when I found this one. Besides, he might just be doing me a favor if he was to get me fired. I might find me something that pays better, and I don't have to get shot at for my money. Ah, to hell with him. What's our next move on this Lang case?"

"It's your case, Elwood."

"Damn it, Rider, I know that. But it's your country and your people we're dealing with. Besides, you got a better head for this sort of thing than I do. Help me out, will you?"

"Well," said Rider, taking out his pipe and tobacco, "you feel up to an all-day horseback ride?"

"When?"

"Leave first thing in the morning."

"Going where?"

"Coyne Fletcher's ranch up in Cooweescoowee District."

Just then George came into the office.

" 'Siyo, George," said Rider. George pulled off his hat and coat and hung them up on the wall pegs. "Where you been all day?"

"Well," said George, "I've been to the National Hotel and out to the seminary. Hello, Elwood. I found Tommy Snail sick in bed at school. Coley Fletcher's hit the trail."

"I figured as much," said Rider.

"It was Coley and Tommy who went through the window, all right," said George. "Well, Tommy didn't go in, but he was with Coley."

"He was waiting with the horses," said Rider.

"Yeah. Coley broke in Chris's office first on Saturday night. He stole an exam and took it back to the hotel to copy."

"He stole what?" said Lovely.

"An exam," said George. "A test. Chris was going to give them a Latin exam, and Coley knew that he couldn't pass it. He stole the exam, took it back to the hotel, and copied it. Here."

He pulled the crumpled paper out of his pocket and handed it to Rider. Rider glanced at it and handed it back, and George took it to Lovely. Lovely squinted at it.

"Latin, huh?" he said.

"Yeah. He meant to copy it and take the original back the same night, but the boys had some whiskey, and Coley had indulged in quite a bit of it. He passed out. Sunday morning he realized that he hadn't put the exam back. He had to go out again on Sunday night. Tommy said that Coley came out of the office in a big hurry. He said that he'd stumbled over Chris's body in the dark."

"So if Tommy's telling the truth," said Lovely, "that means the man with the shoes was there before the boys were. Right?"

"That's right," said George. "The boot prints belong to Coley. The man with the shoes was there first. He killed Chris, took the keys, and put out the light. Then Coley came along and stumbled over the body."

"So Coley Fletcher's not our killer," said Lovely. "We don't need to make that long ride tomorrow."

"I do," said Rider. "He stole a horse. Besides, all we got is Tommy's version of the story, and he never went inside."

"Yeah," said Lovely. "Hell. I guess you're right. I just thought for a minute there that we might get to stay here, where it's warm."

"You riding up to the Fletcher ranch tomorrow?" George asked.

"First thing," said Rider.

"Want me to go along?"

"No. Me and Elwood will be enough, and

likely Dooley will ride on out to the ranch with us. Someone has to stay here and watch over things. We still got old Orren Harkey in there, and now Elwood's got himself two prisoners as well."

"Two?" said George. "Bob Avery and who else?"

"Railroad man name of Winters," said Lovely. "Smart-ass son of a bitch."

"Winters?" said George. "Are you sure?"

"That's what he called himself."

"But that's Councilman Peck's business partner, the man Chris met in Pennsylvania."

"No," said Lovely. "That can't be. Not unless your councilman's in the railroad business. This bastard's a railroad man."

"Where'd you put him?" asked George.

"Right next to Avery. I had them both cussing me at the same time."

"I'll be right back."

George left the office, and Lovely gave Rider a quizzical look.

"What's this all about?" he asked.

Rider shrugged and puffed at his pipe.

"We'll know in a minute," he said.

George came back into the office and stood in the middle of the room.

"Rider," he said, "Elwood, the other morning I had coffee with Chris, and just as we were leaving, Winters came in. Chris spoke to him. Called him by name. Winters tried to ignore him, and Chris even reminded

137

him of where they had met. It was in Philadelphia, when Councilman Peck was bringing
Chris down here to start his job. Peck and
Winters had some kind of meeting. Chris
said he had assumed that they were business
associates."

"And when you told me about it, I assumed that Winters was Peck's eastern business partner," said Rider. "But that ain't
necessarily so."

"He's a goddamned railroad man," said
Lovely. "I told you. I'm sure of it."

"But Councilman Peck's opposed to allowing the railroad to come through the
Cherokee Nation," said George.

"Anyhow that's what he's been leading us
all to believe," said Rider. He recalled the bit
of conversation he had overheard a few days
earlier between Peck and Chief Ross. "If he's
secretly in cahoots with the railroad interests,
that would explain why Winters tried to act
like he didn't know Mr. Lang — he was
trying to hide his association with Peck."

"But Peck slipped up when he let Chris
see him and Winters together in Philadelphia," said George.

"Excuse me just a minute, fellows," said
Lovely, "but tell me if I'm wrong: Ain't you
got council members arguing for both sides
of this fight?"

"Yep, we sure do," said Rider. "Just like on
any other thing that comes up. If someone

138

was to point out the window at the sun in the sky and call it the sun and it was during a council meeting, someone else would get up and call it by another name."

"But if there's members out in the open on both sides," said Lovely, "why would Peck and Winters give a damn if anybody knows what they're up to?"

"Two things I can think of," said Rider. "Them railroad boys is using every trick there is. They've got some of our own boys making speeches on their behalf, but they've also got their spies in the other camp. Looks like Peck is one of them spies."

"You said two things," said Lovely.

"Old Peck's up from Sequoyah District," said Rider. "If the folks down there was to get wind of what he's up to with Winters, they'd toss him out of office right quick. And then if he dared to go back home, they might do worse than that."

Lovely stood up and began to pace. He almost ran into George, who moved quickly over to his desk and sat down to get out of the way.

"This railroad disagreement," said Lovely. "It's serious business, ain't it."

"Yes," said Rider, "it is that."

"Just how serious?"

"Lot of money on the one side," said Rider. "Lot of strong feelings on the other."

"Where there's a lot of money involved,"

said Lovely, "there's motive for murder."

"The shoe prints," said George.

"Winters," said Lovely.

"Or Peck," said Rider. He stood up, picked up his Colts, and tucked them into his pants. "I'm going home," he said.

"What do we do in the morning?" asked Lovely.

"Same as before," said Rider. "You and me'll ride up to Fletcher's. George can stay here and follow up on Peck and Winters. When we all get together again, we'll compare notes and see what we've got."

—13—

George Tanner was alone at the National Prison. Go-Ahead Rider and Elwood Lovely had headed north early. But George didn't mind. He had started his day by stopping at the judge's office, which Rider usually did, and getting a court date for Orren Harkey. He had several other things to do, maybe more than he would be able to get done before the day was over. He drank a cup of coffee in the office and organized his thoughts. Then he went to the cell to see Winters.

The man needed a shave and his fine suit was rumpled, but his manner was as arrogant as ever.

"When are you going to let me out of here?" he demanded.

"Mr. Winters," said George, "even if I wanted to let you out, and I don't, I don't have the authority. You were arrested by an officer of the United States on a violation of a federal law."

"It's ridiculous," said Winters. "No court in the country will convict me on that charge."

"Well, I guess that's what we'll find out,"

said George. "I understand you represent the railroad interests."

"Indeed I do. And I'm personally acquainted with the president of the company as well as with the president of the United States, not to mention numerous congressmen. I can cause a great deal of trouble for you."

"Not for me," said George. "When I first saw you the other morning, I was with Chris Lang. Do you recall that morning?"

"No," said Winters. "I can't say that I do."

"Well, I recall it clearly. Chris and I were on our way out of the café just as you came in. He recognized you, was surprised to see you. He spoke to you and called you by name. You acted like you didn't know him, so he reminded you of when you had met — in Philadelphia, with a member of our council, Mr. Peck. Now do you remember?"

"Yes. It wasn't important to me, that's all. I never knew Mr. Lang."

"But you had met him?"

"Yes, I suppose I must have. I really don't remember the occasion."

"The important thing here is that Chris remembered it," said George. "You see, we all figured that you must have been Mr. Peck's eastern business partner. But you're not his business partner, are you."

"Of course not."

"Then the next question is — what was

the meeting in Philadelphia all about? The meeting between you and Mr. Peck? And just how important was it to you and Peck to keep your association a secret?"

"I don't know what you're talking about."

"I'm talking about the murder of Chris Lang, Mr. Winters."

Winters stiffened. He turned his back on George and stared out the barred window across the cell from him.

"I have nothing more to say to you, Deputy," he said, "and I don't know what you're talking about anyway."

"We'll see," said George. "Right now I'm going to have a talk with Councilman Peck."

As George walked away, Bob Avery, who had been listening carefully to the whole conversation from his cell next to Winters's, jumped up and ran to the bars between the two cells.

"I guess you was telling the truth about being a big shot with the railroad," he said.

"Of course I was telling the truth," said Winters. "What did you think I was? A traveling skunk oil salesman?"

"Don't know what I thought," said Avery. "But I know *something*."

Winters looked over his shoulder at Avery with a sneer on his lips.

"I know that a whiskey warrant's one thing," Avery continued, "and murder's another. Seems to me like the stakes just got higher in this game. What do you say to that? Huh?"

Orren Harkey stepped out the front door of the jail. He stood a moment, reading the slip of paper that George Tanner had given him telling him when he was to report back for his trial. He felt more than a little like he had been treated unjustly, and he wondered what would happen if he simply failed to show up on the appointed day.

All he had done was defend himself. Why, he thought, who took that law against carrying a gun seriously? No one. After all, a man's got to be able to defend himself.

He tucked the paper into a jacket pocket and walked down the stairs. Then he turned to his right and walked around the northeast corner of the building, headed for the creek that ran nearby. Suddenly, he heard his name called in a harsh whisper.

"Orren."

He stopped and looked over his shoulder. There was no one there.

"Orren."

He looked all around. Down the road a small boy was running with a dog. He didn't see anyone else.

"Up here, Orren," said the voice. "In the jail."

He looked up toward the second-floor cell windows and saw Bob Avery's face pressed against the bars and peering down at him.

"What do you want?" he said.

"I want to talk to you," said Avery, "but keep your voice down. I don't want Tanner to hear us."

Harkey walked over closer to the wall and looked up, squinting toward Avery.

"I got nothing to talk to you about," he said. "The last time I talked to you, you pulled a gun on me. The last time I seen you, you was trying to kill me."

"Aw, hey, forget about that," said Avery. "I was drunk. That's all. I'm sorry about all that. You can even have old Suzy; I won't bother you no more about her. Hell, she likes you best anyway."

"You mean that?" said Harkey.

"She told me."

"Well, what do you want with me?"

"I see they let you out. That's good. That damn marshal got me, though. 'Cause I'm a white man."

"Well," said Harkey, shuffling his feet, "I got me a trial date set."

"How would you like to get yourself some money and get out of this country before then?" asked Avery. "They can't have no trial on you if you're somewheres else. What do you say to that?"

Harkey cocked his head to one side and squinted up at Avery.

"I'm listening," he said.

George made one last notation on the list

in front of him. The top item was to locate and interview Mr. Peck. He was curious about how Peck's story would compare with that of Winters. Then he wanted to go through Chris Lang's office and home. There might be some kind of evidence there, although he really didn't think so.

On that score, he was thinking more like a friend than a lawman. Chris's personal effects should be gathered up and shipped to his parents, George felt. He also thought that it was about time he stopped back by the hotel and allowed Sim to clean up the room that Coley Fletcher and Tommy Snail had occupied. Plus he wanted to talk to Tommy again. Then, because he was planning to be out so much of the day, he decided that he should look up Beehunter and enlist him to watch over the jail.

He tucked the note in his pocket, finished off the coffee in his cup, and got up. He put on his hat and coat and left the office. Outside, he shut and locked the main door, and he never knew what hit him. It was Orren Harkey, with a piece of wood he had picked up from under the trees along the creek bank.

George fell like a dropped sack of grain, and Harkey looked around nervously. He didn't see anyone. He dropped to one knee, pulled George's Starr revolver from its holster, and tucked it into the waistband of his trousers. Then he got the key George had dropped when Harkey had clubbed him over the head. He tried the key and unlocked the door. He shoved it open wide, looked around again, then dragged George inside.

Leaving him just inside the door, Harkey ran into the office and found the large ring which held the keys to the cells. He hurried upstairs and found Avery.

"Come on," said Avery. "Get it open."

Harkey fumbled with the keys for a moment, then got one into the door of Avery's cell. It worked. He swung the door open wide. Avery took the keys away from him and unlocked the door to Winters's cell.

"Come on," he said, and the three men went down the stairs and back into the office. They looked through the drawers of Sheriff Rider's desk until they found the things that had been taken away from them at the time of their arrests. Then Avery smashed the door of the gun cabinet and they took a rifle apiece. Avery also took two revolvers for himself and several boxes of cartridges, which he stuffed into his own and his comrades' pockets. Then they hurried out to the main door.

"Hold it," said Harkey. "I'm just going to peek out there and make sure the coast is clear. Then we'll take off to the right. I got three horses hid down in the woods by the creek."

"Where'd you get three horses?" asked Avery.

Harkey grinned.

"Sheriff's barn," he said.

Harkey opened the door and looked out. He saw nothing that bothered him. Winters glanced down at George, lying in the floor by his feet.

"Is he — dead?" he asked.

"I don't know," said Harkey. "I did hit him pretty hard."

"Who gives a shit anyhow?" said Avery.

"The coast is clear," said Harkey. "Come on. Let's go," he commanded, leading the way out of the jail and across Water Street over to where the three saddled horses waited beneath the trees beside the creek. The three men mounted up and rode east toward the Arkansas line.

George Tanner moaned and moved his head a little. His head was throbbing, and he felt as if he were in a deep, dark well. He tried to relax and go back to sleep — or wherever it was he had been — but the pressure of the hard floor against his tender head wouldn't let him. He rolled over and managed to get himself up onto his hands and knees. His head was swimming in a thick fog. At last he sat up and leaned back against the wall, taking his head in his hands.

He still had a powerful impulse to go to sleep, but he knew vaguely that something was wrong. He forced himself to open his eyes and look around. He was in the jail. He was on the floor of the hallway just inside the front door. He tried to think. He remembered that he had been leaving; he had some things to do. He couldn't remember what they were, though. Something about Chris, he thought. Peck. He was going to look for Peck.

No. Beehunter. But why would he want to find Beehunter? Then he remembered Lovely's prisoners in the cells upstairs. He lurched to his feet, and the jail seemed to rock beneath him like the deck of a ship on a stormy sea. He steadied himself and managed to get up the stairs, using the handrails both for balance and for pulling himself along. The cells were empty, their doors standing open. The key ring was on the floor. Prisoners loose, he thought, and he reached for his revolver, but it too was gone. This was real trouble.

He started back down the stairs, but about halfway down his knees buckled under him. He gripped the handrails and managed to get the rest of the way down without falling, then staggered into the office. No one was there, but he saw the smashed door to the gun cabinet, and he noticed that Rider's desk drawers had been pulled out and rifled through. He was lightheaded, and his knees were weak, and he knew that he needed some help.

Leaning against the walls all the way, he went to the front door. It was still standing open. He stepped out, reached for the handrail, missed, and fell headlong down the stairs.

When George woke up again, he was in his own bed. Lee was there mopping his brow with a damp cloth.

"George," she said. "Oh, George, are you all right?"

"I don't know," he said. "How'd I get here?"

As his eyes began to focus more clearly, he noticed Exie Rider standing on the far side of the room. She was holding little Rider Tanner.

"Somebody found you in the yard in front of the jail," said Lee. "They ran for the doctor. He brought you here in a wagon. Exie came along with him. I guess maybe he took you to his office first. Oh, I don't remember what all he said."

George reached up and touched the side of his head. He felt a bandage there, and beneath it, his head felt tender to his touch. He winced.

"What's this?" he said.

"You've had a very hard blow to the head," said Lee. "What happened? Who did it?"

"I don't know. I remember starting to leave the office. I went out and locked the door.

That's all I remember. That must be when it happened. But then . . ."

"What?" said Lee.

"I woke up back inside. I checked the cells, and the prisoners were gone. They took some guns from the office, too. Lee, I've got to get up."

George tried to raise himself, but Lee put her hands on his chest and held him down. He didn't have the strength to resist her.

"No you don't," she said. "The doctor said you're to lie still. Whatever's wrong out there, it can wait until Rider gets back."

"No," said George. "No, it can't wait. Rider and Elwood won't be back until to-morrow evening. I've got to go find Beehunter."

Exie stepped toward the bed.

"Jaji," she said, "just be still. Here, Lee, take little Rider. I'll go find Beehunter."

—14—

Beehunter had his own rifle and ammunition. He also had his own horse. It was a good thing, too — the men he was pursuing had cleaned out the gun cabinet in the sheriff's office and the horse stalls in the sheriff's barn. Beehunter had no way of knowing if he would be paid for his work that day. In order to hire "special deputies," as they were called, Rider had to first get official approval. But when Rider needed help, Beehunter was always ready and willing, and Exie knew that.

She had gone to his house and told him there was trouble, and then he had gone with her to the Tanner home. George had told him — through Exie, for Beehunter could speak and understand only Cherokee — about the events of the day. So Beehunter knew that he was looking for three men: two escaped prisoners and a third man who had helped them escape, the one who had hit George. He knew that the two escapees were white men and federal prisoners and that therefore he had no authority over them, even if his deputization was legal, and he wasn't at all sure about that.

But those things did not concern

Beehunter. He went to the jail, and he went to the sheriff's barn, and he found where three horses had been taken from the barn and led to a place in the nearby woods. He followed the tracks of the three horses out to the road, where they were lost in the tracks of other traffic. But they had headed for the north edge of town. If they continued north, they would go into the Delaware District of the Cherokee Nation. That didn't make any sense to Beehunter. But just a little north of town, they could turn east and go toward Arkansas. Beehunter headed for the Arkansas road.

When Coley Fletcher had arrived at his home, his father had come out onto the porch of the big ranch house. Coley had hoped that Coyne would be out somewhere, and that he could put the horse away and change his clothes before he had to face the old man. But it had been too late. There he'd stood, watching Coley ride in. So the boy had gone straight to the porch, stopped, and dismounted.

Coyne Fletcher had so many questions, he didn't know which one to ask first. Whose horse was his son riding, and why was the boy such a mess? What was he doing at home on a Monday when he should be in school? Whatever the answers to those questions, he figured they would all add up to some kind of trouble.

"What's wrong, boy?" he said.

"It's a long story, Dad."

Coyne looked toward the corral and saw a cowhand working there.

"Slim," he shouted, "come over here and take care of this horse." Then he spoke to Coley again. "Come on inside," he said. "Get yourself cleaned up, and then you can tell me all about it."

Coley had been surprised to find his father so calm. He had expected a raging storm, and it occurred to him that the storm could still be building and would descend on him with full force a little later. He went into the house, said hello to his mother, and went to his room. He washed and put on clean clothes. When he reappeared in the main part of the house, his mother fed him. Only then did Coyne speak again.

"Come on over here and sit down," he said.

Coley took an easy chair across from where his father sat. He tried to smile, but he only managed a sheepish grin.

"It's Monday," said Coyne.

"Yes sir," said Coley. He looked over his shoulder toward his mother for support, but she was just standing there, a worried expression on her face. "I know."

"Why aren't you at school? Is it some sort of holiday?"

Coley thought about telling a lie, but he couldn't figure out where to start. It had all seemed so simple — just copy the exam and make a grade — but it had led to an incredible mess that he could see no way out of. There was nothing to do but tell the truth, however painful that might be.

"No sir. No holiday. I got myself into a passel of trouble," he said. "It was stupid, but I done it, and I can't undo it now."

"Tell me about it, son," said Coyne.

"There was a Latin exam coming up. It was to be on Wednesday. I knew I couldn't pass it, and I was scared of what you'd say, so I decided to cheat."

"Coley," said Mrs. Fletcher. Coyne raised a hand for silence, and she obeyed.

"Well," said Coley, "the only way I could figure to cheat was to copy the questions, so I went into the teacher's office at night and stole the exam. Just so I could copy it."

Mrs. Fletcher pulled a chair away from the table and sat down.

"How'd you get in?" said Coyne.

"Through the window. It was dark, and I didn't want to put on a light in the office, so I took the exam to a hotel room, and I copied it there. I meant to put it back that same night, but I fell asleep and didn't wake up until daylight. So I went back Sunday night, and I went back in through the window again. Just like before. I put it back, all right, but then I tripped over something. It was Mr. Lang, my teacher, and he was dead, and I got his blood on me. Well, I had a rented horse, and I just lit out for home. That's about it."

"Coley," said his father, "did you kill that man?"

"No sir. I swear I never. I stumbled over his dead body, and that's all."

"If that's all," said Coyne, his brow knit in deep thought, "you should've just gone on to school like nothing was wrong. No one would have known the difference. Now they'll wonder where you are. Why you're not in school. And there's that horse out there. They'll be looking for him. You were all right until you run off."

Coley looked at the floor. Nervously, he rubbed his thighs with his hands.

"Well, no sir. I wasn't," he said. "Not really. I had blood all over my jacket, and back at the hotel, I laid down on the bed. It was dark and I didn't realize what I was doing. But I got blood on the sheets. In the morning when I seen them sheets, and when I seen how bad it was on my clothes, I just took them sheets and got the hell out of there. And there was another boy with me too. I don't know if he'll talk or not. I told him not to, but I don't know."

Coyne Fletcher stood up and paced the floor.

"What else have you left out of your story?" he said.

"Nothing, Dad," said Coley. "Anyway, I *think* I've told you everything. I might've forgot something. I don't know. Hell."

"Coley," said Mrs. Fletcher, "you watch your language in this house."

"Yes ma'am," said Coley. "Sorry."

"I had such big plans for you, boy," said Coyne. "Where did I go wrong? All this money I've made — it was so you could make something of yourself, be somebody important. A lawyer maybe. I never went to more than the fourth grade in school, and I had to scratch and claw for everything I got. But I wanted you to have more than that. I wanted you to have a better chance than what I'd had. Get a better start. Now you've ruined it. You've ruined it all."

"Dad," said Coley, "I know what you wanted, but I ain't cut out for school. I don't like it, and I ain't no good at it. And I don't want to be no lawyer, either. There's only one thing I ever wanted to be. I just wanted to grow up to be like you. I just wanted to be the biggest and best rancher in the whole Cherokee Nation. That's all. Just like you. And you *have* given me a better start than you had. You've got this ranch, and you raised me on it and taught me how to run it. That's all I want. It's all I ever wanted."

Coyne Fletcher's eyes teared up, so he

157

looked off in the other direction. He had never known that his son looked up to him like that. He wondered why, until serious trouble forced the issue, he had never found a way or the time to sit down and talk with the boy and find out these things about him. He pulled a handkerchief out of his pocket and wiped his eyes.

"Coley," he said, looking at his son again, "don't worry. They can kick you out of school for what you done, but that's all. They can't put you in jail for something you didn't do. I won't let that happen."

He turned to leave the house, but he was stopped by a word from his wife.

"Coyne," she said, "where you going?"

"I'm going out to set some guards on the road," he said.

The guards stood watch the rest of that day and all through the night, with the shifts continuing into the next day. "Don't let no strangers in," Coyne Fletcher had ordered, "and no lawmen. If they won't turn back when you tell them to, shoot them."

Avery had set a fast pace as soon as the three riders had gotten themselves clear of Tahlequah. Then he slowed them down.

"These horses won't never make it to the line if we run them too hard," he said.

"Are you sure we're not being followed?" asked Winters.

"No," said Avery. "I ain't sure. But you wanted out of that jail, didn't you?"

"Of course."

"Well, you're out. Now just don't forget what you promised me."

"You'll be taken care of," said Winters. "Don't worry. Just get me to a railroad."

Winters was uncomfortable. He could control the horse, but he was not a good rider. He did not sit well in the saddle. It seemed as if every time the horse went down, he went up, and then his rear end and the saddle would meet again with a slap. He sweated, in spite of the cold air, and he breathed in puffs and pants. He was used to much finer accommodations.

He was also wondering what he would do with his new acquaintances once they reached a railroad. He could pay them off and send them on their way. That would work with Harkey, he was sure. But he was also sure that Avery had bigger ideas, like a high-paying job with the railroad, one where he didn't have to work.

Maybe he would have to take Avery along with him, as distasteful as the thought was. He could secure a job of some kind for the man, let him lounge around for a while and then get him fired. What else could he do? Here in this wild Indian Territory, Winters thought, he was at their mercy. He needed Avery, at least, to guide him to safety. And besides that, if Avery believed that he was trying to double-cross him, Winters had no doubt, the scoundrel would kill him in a minute. Still, he said to himself, he would sure like to think of some way to get rid of both Avery and Harkey before getting on the train.

"Hold up a minute," said Harkey.

"What for?" asked Avery.

"This horse has gone lame."

Avery dismounted and examined the horse on which Harkey had been riding.

"Well, hell," he said, "I can't tell what's wrong with him, but he sure as hell is favoring that right foreleg. Pull the saddle off him and throw it over there beside the road. I guess you and me'll just have to double up."

Avery climbed back up onto his horse as Harkey busied himself unsaddling the other. Winters looked nervously back down the road toward Tahlequah. Harkey pulled the saddle off the back of the lame horse and, turning his back on Avery, walked toward the edge of the road.

Winters gasped slightly as he saw Avery slip the revolver out of the holster at his side. He aimed it at Harkey's back and thumbed the hammer. Harkey heard the clicks. He stopped. He dropped the saddle and turned, clawing at the revolver stuck in his pants. Avery's gun roared and a hole opened up in Harkey's chest. He died on his feet and slowly crumpled down into the dust of the road.

"Good Lord," said Winters.

"He'd have just slowed us down," said Avery, "and cost you more money. We don't need him no more anyhow. Let's get going."

It was late evening when Go-Ahead Rider and Elwood Lovely arrived at a small settlement not far from the Fletcher ranch in the Cooweescoowee District of the Cherokee Nation.

"I don't think we ought to ride out there this late," Rider said. "I think we ought to stop here for the night and go out there first thing in the morning, when we're rested."

"I'll go along with that," said Lovely. "Where do we stay? Someplace warm, I hope."

"Sheriff Dooley, district sheriff up here, lives right over there. He'll put us up. He'll also ride out to the ranch with us in the morning."

"That's fine with me," said Lovely, "just as long as he's got a fire going."

Beehunter knew the country between Tahlequah and the Arkansas line as well as anyone. He had hunted every inch of it for most of his life, hunted deer, squirrel, quail, possum, and man. He had no intention of staying on the road and trailing behind the fugitives, or of taking a chance on killing his horse by trying to catch up with them. He knew where they were going; at least he thought that he did. They were staying on the road and heading for the Arkansas line. And he knew a shorter way, a way that would take him across the rugged, forested hills and bring him out on the road ahead of them. He took that trail.

It was a steep climb at first, and then it was a treacherous trail through thick woods, but Beehunter was familiar with it. He knew where the trail seemed to come to an end and he would have to ride around a thick tangle of bramble to locate where it picked up again on the other side. He knew where the rocks were loose on the hillsides and he had to go slow and careful, and he knew where the trail widened and leveled off enough so that he could pick up the pace and make good time.

When he arrived at the other end, the sun was already low in the western sky, but Beehunter knew that he had gotten out in front of the fugitives. The Arkansas line was just ahead. He figured they would be along in something less than an hour. He left his horse in the woods to his back and settled himself in behind some big boulders on the side of the hill. He had a good view of the road below. He laid his rifle across a rock and settled in to wait.

—15—

The rifle crack in the morning stillness startled the horses. Avery managed to keep in the
saddle, but Winters fell off backward as his
horse reared, and he landed hard on the road.
It hurt him — his back was bruised and all
the air was knocked out of his lungs. Avery
pulled out his revolver and looked around
nervously for something to shoot back at.

"Hlesdi," Beehunter called out from behind
his rock hideaway.

Avery fired a wild shot in the direction of
the voice, vaulted from his horse's back, and
scampered for the edge of the road. The
brush was tall and thick there, and he
crashed into it, burrowing deep.

"Shit," he said as the bramble scratched his
face and hands. "Ow. Damn."

"Avery?" said Winters, still gasping for
breath. "Avery. What's going on? Where are
you?"

He had caught his breath, but he was still
lying on his back in the road, afraid to move.

"Get off the road and hide your fat ass,"
said Avery. "You make a hell of a good target
out there like that."

With effort, Winters rolled over on his

163

belly and got up to his hands and knees. He remembered the awful hole in Harkey's chest, and he kept expecting to feel a bullet burn into his own too soft flesh.

"Get off the road," he muttered. "Yes. Yes, of course. Get off the road."

He crawled for the tangle of brush. Up on the hillside behind the big rocks, Beehunter let Winters go. The other one was the problem, he knew. If he could get the gunfighter, the fat white man would come crawling back out with his hands high in the air. Let him hide for now, Beehunter said to himself.

Anyhow, he did not want to kill these men unless he had to. Had he wanted to kill them, his first shot would have killed Avery. It would have been easy. Then he could have shot the fat man while he floundered on his back in the dirt. He wanted to stop them and take them back to jail, alive if possible. If they wouldn't cooperate, well, he would kill them, but only if they forced him to.

"Avery?"

Winters called out in a harsh whisper from his rat hole in the brush and weeds. He was still panting. He was sore from the horseback ride and bruised from his fall. He had not counted on anything like this. Even in his youth he had not been a great physical specimen, and he was no longer young. He worried about his heart.

"Avery?"

"What?"

"Who is that?"

"I ain't asked him," said Avery, "and I sure ain't had a good look at him, but I think it's that deputy of Rider's, the one that can't talk English. He told us to stop in Cherokee."

"Well, talk to him," said Winters. "Find out what he wants."

"I can't talk Cherokee," said Avery. "I recognized that one word, that's all. Besides, I know what he wants. He wants to take us back to jail. That's what he wants. Either that or kill us."

It didn't make sense to Winters. Avery admitted that he couldn't understand the man's language. He hadn't gotten a look at him, either. It might not be the deputy, as far as Winters could tell. It might be a road agent. It could be anyone.

"Hello," he called out. "You up there. Can you hear me?"

He received an answer, but the words were unintelligible to him.

"Who are you?" he called out. "What do you want with us? If you want money, I don't have any with me, but I can get you some. I can get you a lot of money. Just come down and stop shooting at us. Let's work something out. All right?"

He heard some more of the strange language, and then he heard the taunting voice of Bob Avery.

"He don't understand a word you're saying, Winters. Save your breath. It's that damn full-blooded deputy for sure. That's who it is."

Beehunter, he thought. That's what they call that son of a bitch. Beehunter. He tried to think of a way to draw Beehunter out so he could get a shot at him, but the only schemes he could bring to mind all involved saying something, and all depended on the other party's being able to understand what was being said.

If only he had his rifle; then he could stand up, hands over his head, rifle in hand, and toss the rifle down. It would look like a surrender. Beehunter would start down the hill, and then Avery could quickly draw his revolver and shoot. But the rifle was in the saddle boot on the horse, out in the middle of the road.

He looked out at the horses, studying their positions in the road. They were still a bit nervous, but they had not run off. His mount had turned and trotted a few paces back to mill around near the other. Avery wondered just where Winters was in relation to them. If the horses were between Winters and Beehunter, Winters might be able to get to one of the rifles without exposing himself to Beehunter's line of fire.

If he could help it, Avery did not want to get Winters killed. The man was his ticket to a fortune and a life of comfort and ease. But if the choice turned out to be between fortune and life, Avery would, of course, choose life. He would sacrifice Winters if he had to. In a minute.

"Winters," he said.

"What?"

"Where are you?"

"Now how am I supposed to answer that?" said Winters. "I'm in the bushes. Like you. If you're facing our mysterious opponent, then I'm somewhere to your immediate right."

"Are you close to them horses?"

"Why, uh, yes. They're right in front of me."

"See if you can get out there and get that rifle. You see it?"

"Yes, I see it, but I'm not going out there. I could get killed."

"The horses are in his way if he tries to shoot you," said Avery. "They're between him and you. You can make it."

"No," said Winters. "I won't do it. I'm not a gunfighter."

"Damn it, Winters," said Avery, "he's got a rifle up there. All I've got is just a six-shooter. It's no match. Can't you understand that? He's going to get us sooner or later. Unless you can bring me that rifle."

"I'll give myself up," said Winters. "He won't shoot me if I surrender."

"Then you'll hang, you dumb son of a

bitch. Remember that deputy? He was dead. So is Harkey."

"I didn't do it. I didn't kill either one of them."

"You ever heard of a sessory? You dumb shit. You'll hang anyway, just the same as if you'd killed them yourself. Now go get me a rifle, damn you."

Winters's heart pounded in his chest — dangerously, he thought. What were his choices? Surrender? He would be taken back to jail, and in addition to the whiskey charges, he would be charged with jailbreaking. He might even be charged as an accessory to murder, as Avery had said. He did not know whether the sheriff's deputy back at the jail had been unconscious or dead, but there was poor Harkey back down the road, and he was dead for sure. And then there were the horses. Were they stolen? Most likely, he thought. Yes. Yes, they were. He remembered. Harkey had said that he had gotten them from the sheriff's barn. He wasn't sure about the law, but he had heard that they hung horse thieves out in the West. No. He did not want to go back to jail. He did not want to hang. Avery was right: He could not afford to surrender.

He could lie still and do nothing, but eventually something was bound to happen. Avery had just said that without the rifle, they would be captured. Or killed. He could turn around and keep crawling through the brush, get away from the deputy and from Avery, leave Avery to fight it out with the deputy. But where would he go? He didn't even know where he was. How would he ever find his way back to civilization? He could freeze to death or starve or be eaten by some wild animal.

His only other choice seemed to be to do as Avery had told him to. He took a deep breath and inched forward, certain that the lawman on the hill could hear the rustling of the brush and see the movement. Each motion he made sent shocks of pain through his tortured body. Sooner than he expected, though, he was back at the edge of the road.

Beehunter saw the fat man poke his nose out of the weeds, the way a rat will peek out of a hole before coming all the way out to expose himself. He watched. The man crept out, all the way onto the road, on his hands and knees. Then he stood up in a low crouch and looked around nervously. Beehunter waited to see what the man was up to.

The man moved toward the horses. Was he going to try to mount up and escape? That would be foolish. As he approached the near horse, it whickered, stamped around a bit, and danced backward, away from the man. The man moved on quickly to the second horse and reached for the saddle. Beehunter raised his rifle and sighted in. But no; the man was not going to try to mount up and run away. He was reaching for a rifle. Beehunter fired into the ground just in front of the horse. The horse reared and neighed. The man dropped immediately to his knees, trembling, and covered his head with his arms.

"No. No," he shouted. "Don't shoot. Don't kill me."

Avery raised himself from the bushes as Beehunter showed himself in order to make his shot. He raised his revolver and snapped off a round. It chipped rock just to Beehunter's right. Avery thumbed back the hammer for a second shot, but Beehunter was quicker. He cranked another shell into the chamber, swung the rifle barrel around, and squeezed the trigger.

Avery only had time for a brief astonishment. He did not even pull the trigger. His eyes opened wide and his mouth fell open as the slug tore into his chest. He leaned backward and hesitated a moment as his hand went limp and the revolver fell from his fingers. Then, life and balance failing him at the same moment, he toppled over into the brush.

Beehunter came down the hill. He could hear the blubbering of Winters, but, of course, he had no idea what the man was saying. He tied Winters's hands behind his back and made him sit down in the road. Then he got the reins of the nearest horse and looped them around one of the arms of his captive. He caught up the other horse and did the same with it. Then he dragged the body of Avery out of the brush and loaded it onto the back of one of the animals.

He knew he had tied Winters well, but taking no chances, he gathered up the guns and ran back up the hill to the woods behind the rocks, where he had left his mount. He led it down to the road. Then he pulled Winters to his feet, loosed the reins from around his arm, shoved him up into the saddle, and, taking the reins of both of the fugitives' horses in his hand, swung up into his own saddle and turned them all back toward Tahlequah.

He had not seen any sign of the third man, and so he knew that he would have to be watchful. The man might have dropped off along the way to watch their back trail for any pursuit. If so, he would be looking to-ward Tahlequah, not toward Arkansas, but Beehunter would still have to be careful not to run up on the man unexpectedly.

It was about the middle of the day when he found the limping horse and not far away, beside the road, the body of Orren Harkey. Winters began blabbering again, but Beehunter couldn't understand him, so he paid no attention. He checked the foot of the lame horse and found that it had only picked up a rock; it would be all right. He knocked the rock loose and loaded Harkey's body onto the horse's back. Then, confident that he had all three fugitives, he resumed the trip back to Tahlequah, fully relaxed.

—16—

George was back in the office, in spite of the protests of Lee and Exie. Rider was gone to Cooweescoowee District looking for young Coley Fletcher, and Beehunter was on the trail of the escapees. No one was left at the office, and so, after he had rested a while, George had gotten out of bed and gone back to work. He had told Lee that he was all right, but he knew that he would be in trouble if he had to do anything as strenuous as run a few steps. He still felt a little light-headed and dizzy.

Lee was worried about him. He had taken a pretty hard blow to the head, and she wasn't at all sure that he should even be out of his bed, much less back at work. She had argued with him, but he had insisted.

"Rider depends on me," he had said. "And we've got a murderer out loose somewhere. Chris's murderer. I can't just lie around in bed."

Little Rider had finished his nap and Lee had fed him. He was back in his crib playing with a small toy that Beehunter had carved for him shortly after his birth. It had a little ball inside a compartment. The fit was tight, but the ball was loose enough to move. The sides were open so that the ball could be seen rolling up and down as the toy was tilted, and if it was shaken hard enough, it rattled a bit. Little Rider was shaking it.

Lee tried to busy herself in the kitchen, but she had really already taken care of everything there. She was relieved when she heard the knock at the door, and she rushed to open it.

"Exie," she said, surprised. "Come in."

"I sent my kids over to my sister's house when they came home from school," said Exie. "I thought maybe you might need some help."

"I appreciate it," said Lee, "but I don't really. I've just been looking for something to do to keep myself busy around here. George went back to the office."

"He shouldn't be out of bed," said Exie, astonished.

"I tried to stop him, but he wouldn't listen to me."

"Well," said Exie, "let's go down there and see him."

Lee hesitated, glancing toward little Rider in his crib.

"We can bring him along with us," said Exie. "I brought a buggy. Just wrap him up real good. It's a little bit cold outside."

George was at his desk writing a letter.

There were several things that he thought he should be doing, but most of them required that he leave the office, and he wasn't sure he should do that. He didn't want to leave it unattended, and he wasn't really sure that he was up to much running around.

One of the things he had been meaning to do was write a letter to Chris Lang's parents. He didn't know their names or their address, but he thought he might be able to find that information later. He might find it among Chris's things. If not, the school might have it in Chris's file. In the meantime, while he was just passing time in the office, he could at least compose the letter. It wasn't easy. He began:

Dear Mr. and Mrs. Lang,

It is my very painful duty to have to inform you of the death of your son Chris. In the relatively short time since his arrival here in our town, Chris and I had become good friends, and I find that I am missing his company very much.

Chris was —

He heard the front door being opened, and he put the letter away in his desk drawer. It wasn't the sort of thing he would want anyone else to even glance at. It was too personal and too painful, and the writing of it made George feel clumsy and awkward. He sat up straight in his chair and watched the office door to see who would come in.

"Lee," he said, surprised by his wife's sudden appearance. Then the surprise was doubled. "Exie. What are you two doing here?"

"We came to check up on you, Jaji," said Exie. "It was my idea too, so don't fuss at your wife."

"Well," said George, "I — I'm all right."

"You don't look all right to me," said Exie. "You're trying to get up and around way too quick. You should be home in bed."

"Exie," said George, "I went over all that with Lee already. Rider's out of town, probably for two days. We've sent Beehunter out — without authorization, really, but we've got escapees out there somewhere. We're working on a murder case, and I don't dare put on another special deputy. I'm the only one here."

"It won't hurt for this place to be locked up for a day or two," said Exie.

"No, Exie," said George. "I know you're trying to help, and I appreciate it, but I can't just close down the National Prison because I have a little headache."

"Aha," said Lee. "Your head does still hurt. You just admitted it."

"Lee."

"Tell you what," said Exie. "I'll go over there and talk to Judge Boley and see if he wants to lock up the jailhouse or put on another deputy, just till Rider gets back. You go on back home."

"No," said George. "I really appreciate your concern, but look, even if I could get out of the office, there are other things I should be doing. I really should get over to Chris Lang's house and to his office and go through his things. I've already put it off too long as it is."

"Why do you need to go through Chris's things?" asked Lee.

"I don't know," said George. "Someone has to. It's part of the routine. Some of his personal things will most likely be sent to his parents. I don't know; it's just something that has to be done. He has no family here. I'm not really looking forward to it, but —"

"We could do that for you," said Exie.

"You?"

"Yes," she said, gesturing toward Lee. "The two of us."

George hesitated.

"I don't know," he said.

But Exie hurried over to the capitol anyway and had a talk with Judge Harm Boley. She returned to the prison in a few minutes. Delbert Swim would be arriving at the jail soon with authorization to serve as special deputy until Rider's return. Exie then persuaded Lee to ride with her to her sister's house and to leave little Rider there, and she made George promise to at least lie down in the jail as soon as Swim arrived.

Before long, Exie and Lee were in Lang's office at the seminary. They had checked in with Mr. Downing, the principal, of course, and told him their intentions. He had unlocked the office for them and left them there alone. The two women stood in the middle of the room, looking around.

"What do we look for?" asked Exie.

"I guess we'll just sort of get everything organized," said Lee. "You know, stack all the books up together and then all the loose paper. Put the odds and ends in one desk drawer maybe. George will want to look through it all eventually and decide what to box up and send to Chris's parents."

So Exie stacked books while Lee sat at the desk and went through papers. The material that was obviously part of a specific course, she put together in one pile; someone would have to take over the classes, and whoever it might be would want to see what had gone on before. She hesitated for a moment over a paper written by Lang himself. It was an analysis of literary devices used by Cicero, and all of the examples were given in the original Latin.

For a moment she longed for her teaching days. Her career had been a short one. She had met George and married him after a brief courtship. Not long afterward, she had learned that she was carrying a child. At the end of the school year, she had resigned.

She read a few paragraphs of the paper on Cicero, feeling the scholar in her trying to come out again. Then she laid it aside.

"You know, Exie," she said, "he was a brilliant young man. It's really a shame."

"I wonder who killed him," said Exie.

"And why," added Lee. "Why would anyone want to harm such a nice man? I just don't understand it at all."

"Rider said that they found a few with reasons," said Exie.

"Well, yes, I guess they did."

"That Fletcher boy," said Exie. "That's where Rider's gone today. To find that Fletcher boy."

"And there's Willit Barnes," said Lee. "He and Chris had a fight."

"Over a girl. Girls can always give nice young men a reason to fight. Maybe to kill."

"Umm, you're probably right," said Lee. She rummaged through some more papers, placing them in the appropriate stacks. "Exie, has Rider talked to you much about this case?"

"Oh, yeah. Some. He said it ain't his case really. It belongs to the U.S."

"George told me that Rider doesn't really believe that any of their suspects is the guilty one."

"Yeah, he did say something like that. He

thinks there must be somebody else, someone they ain't found out about yet."

"Yes. I wonder if there might not be some hint among Chris's papers. Something that would give us an idea, you know?" Lee moved some more papers. Then she picked up a small notepad. "Kenyon College," she read out loud.

"What?" said Exie.

"That's all it says. Kenyon College." She held up the pad for Exie to see, and Exie shrugged. Lee laid the notepad aside by itself. It wasn't much longer before the two women had everything in the office organized. Then they reported to the principal's office.

"All through, ladies?" asked Downing.

"We've organized everything so that when George comes by later he'll be able to look it over pretty quickly," said Lee. "And all the papers for each different class are in separate piles. Whoever you find to finish the courses up may want to look at them."

"Thank you," said Downing. "I'm sure he will. Well, I'd better go lock the door then, if you're finished in there."

"Yes," said Lee. "We're finished. Oh, Mr. Downing."

"Yes?"

"Does Kenyon College mean anything to you? Mr. Lang left this note here. That's all it says. Kenyon College. It's probably not important, but I just thought it was curious."

Downing looked at the notepad Lee was holding up.

"Well, uh, yes, as a matter of fact. It does ring a bell. Mr. Lang asked me not long ago where Mr. Morrison had been before he came here."

"Kenyon College?"

"Yes. Mr. Morrison came to us, with a modest letter of recommendation, from Kenyon College."

"Thank you, Mr. Downing," said Lee.

From the seminary, Exie drove to the home of Chris Lang's landlord and got him to open the house that Lang had rented. He cooperated because he knew that the women were the wives of the two lawmen, and he, of course, had heard about the murder.

"Are they going to get all this stuff out of here?" he asked. "I need to clean the place up and see if I can rent it out again."

"It won't be long now, I'm sure," said Lee. "Thank you. We'll let you know when we're through."

He took the hint and left, and again Lee and Exie started to sort and pile. This time, though, they found themselves sorting clothes, personal effects, and household items. There were but a few books and papers in the small house.

"He obviously did most of his work at the office," said Lee.

"Rider don't bring things home from work either," said Exie.

"No. Neither does George. But we do read at home."

"There's books here."

"Yes. A few."

Lee opened a bureau drawer and found some letters. She glanced at the return address and knit her brow.

"George will want to see these," she said.

"What is it?" asked Exie.

"Letters from Chris's parents, I believe."

She took them out of the drawer and carried them to a small table that sat against the wall beside the door.

"I'll just put them here so we'll remember to take them with us," she said. She put the letters down and went back to the bureau. She opened other drawers and found nothing of particular interest, so she started to consolidate the items into one drawer. Exie was stripping the bed and folding up the bedclothes.

"What's this?" Exie said.

"What?"

"Little book here on the nightstand."

Exie put down the blanket she was folding and picked up the book, then opened the cover.

"It ain't a printed book," she said. "It's all in handwriting."

Lee moved across the room to Exie's side to get a look at the book.

"It's a diary, I think," she said.

"Here," said Exie, handing the book to Lee. "I can't read it."

Lee took the book and went to a chair to sit down and read.

"Yes," she said. "It is a diary. Or a journal. It looks like Chris wrote something in it just about every day. Oh, listen to this. 'Today I met George Tanner, a Cherokee of mixed blood and a deputy sheriff of this district. He's a likeable fellow, and the real surprise is this: He has a degree in the classics from Harvard. I think we're going to be great friends.' Oh, Exie."

Exie stepped over to put a hand on Lee's shoulder as Lee flipped a few pages. She turned toward the end of the entries, and then she stopped turning pages and read again. She sat up straight.

"Exie," she said, "the rest of this can wait. We've got to get this journal to George. Right now."

—17—

When Lee and Exie returned to the sheriff's office, they found George, not sleeping on the cot in the room next to the office, not even resting there, but sitting behind his desk writing. Well, Lee thought, at least he's not out running around. She put the letters on his desk in front of him.

"I thought you might want to see these," she said.

George picked up the bundle of letters and glanced at them, noticing right away who had sent them.

"Yes," he said. "Thank you. As a matter of fact, I've just finished composing a letter to Chris's parents, and I needed their names and address. I'm glad you found these."

Lee put a hand on George's shoulder.

"I know that must have been difficult," she said, "writing that letter. There's something else, though."

"Oh? What is it?"

Lee put the notepad with "Kenyon College" on its front page and the journal on the desk in front of George.

"I think," she said, "you'll find these very interesting."

George picked up the journal and opened it up to read.

"What is this?" he said.

"It's a journal," said Lee. "Like a diary. It looks to me like Chris wrote in it almost every day. You need to look at the last few pages."

George was thumbing through the journal when the door to the office was opened and Willit Barnes stepped in. He would have looked somewhat improved since George had seen him last, except that his face wore a long, haggard expression. Lee and Exie stepped out of the way. George stood up.

"Willit?" he said. "What is it? What can I do for you?"

"I come to turn myself in, Deputy," said Willit.

"Turn yourself in?" said George.

Willit gave a short nod of his head.

"You'll want to be locking me up now," he said.

"What for?"

"I killed him."

"You killed him?" asked George, incredulous. "What for?"

"The beating," said Willit. "It just got to be too much to take. And I killed him."

George went across the room for the straight chair, which he placed next to his desk.

"Here, Willit," he said. "Sit down."

Willit sat in the chair, and George went

back to the seat behind his desk.

Lee glanced at Exie. She was desperately curious about Willit's abrupt confession, but she was also very much aware that she was intruding. Exie must have felt the same way, for she whispered to Lee, "We better go now."

"George," said Lee, "excuse me, but I think Exie and I should leave now. Her two and our little Rider are all at her sister's house, and I think we should give the poor woman some relief. You read that journal when you get a chance."

"Yes," said George. "I will. And thank you, ladies, for your help today."

Just then Delbert Swim opened the door to the office. He almost ran into Exie, who was leading the way out. He stopped and stepped back out of the way

"Excuse me," he said.

" *'Siyo,* Del," said Exie.

"We were just on our way out," said Lee. "I'm glad you're here. George has had a rough day here alone."

"Yes ma'am," said Swim. "I heard. I'm glad to be here, ma'am."

"Good-bye now," said Lee.

"Good-bye, ma'am . . . Mrs. Rider."

The ladies left, and Swim stepped on into the office. He saw George sitting at his small desk and Willit Barnes just beside it. Willit was staring straight ahead, not seeming to be looking at anything. Swim could tell that all was not right. He nodded a greeting toward George, and George acknowledged it with a gesture, his attention staying with Willit. Swim moved quietly around the edge of the room, winding up in Rider's chair behind the big desk.

"Willit," said George, "are you telling me that you killed Chris Lang just because he whipped you in front of Hannah Girty?"

"What?" said Willit. "Lang? The school-teacher? No. I never done that. I'm talking about my old man. I just killed my old man."

"Oh God," said George. "Your father? You killed your father?"

"Yes sir. I did. That's what I come here to turn myself in for."

George sucked in a deep breath and then blew it out audibly.

"How did you do it, Willit?" he asked.

"I turned his own shotgun on him. He was laying there in his bed, and I just shot him. That's all."

"Where's the — Where is he now?"

"Just there, I guess."

"In the bed?"

"Yes sir. Just where I left him."

"And your mother, Willit. Where is she?"

"I guess she's there; I don't know where she'd go. I told her I was coming here. She was home when I left."

George turned toward Delbert Swim.

"Delbert," he said, "do you know Willit Barnes here?"

"Yeah," said Swim, self-conscious. "Sure. I know him. How you doing, Willit?"

"Willit just told me that he's killed his father."

"Yeah. I heard," said Swim.

"I'm going to have to ride out there to the house now," said George. "Would you put Willit in a cell?"

"Sure," said Swim. "Sure."

He got the big key ring off its hook and stepped over to Willit, putting a hand on his shoulder.

"You, uh, you want to come along with me, Willit?" he said.

Willit didn't answer. He just stood up and turned to walk ahead of Delbert Swim toward the cells.

The journal was still on George's desktop when he rode out toward Dog Town. He found the body and talked to the grieving widow, but he was not certain whether she was grieving for her dead husband or for her jailed son. He had the body taken care of and went back to the office to finish the paperwork on Willit. Soon afterwards, Beehunter rode in.

He had one live prisoner and two dead bodies. He told his story to Swim, who translated his Cherokee into English for George. George turned to Winters, slumped in a chair against the wall. He was a mess — dirty, bruised and scratched. He looked exhausted, and he looked scared.

"Mr. Winters," he said, "I want to remind you that you're the prisoner of Deputy United States Marshal Lovely. I'm putting you back in a cell here in the Cherokee National Prison just as a courtesy to Mr. Lovely. Do you understand that?"

Winters nodded his head slowly.

"Yes," he said. He appeared to be a beaten man.

"I'm also going to inform Mr. Lovely," said George, "that you were a part of a prison break, during the course of which an officer of the law was assaulted and a citizen of the Cherokee Nation was murdered. Mr. Winters, you'd have been much better off if you'd just waited quietly in the cell and taken what was coming to you on the whiskey charge. With your connections you could probably have beaten it, or at least gotten off with a small fine.

"Delbert, would you lock him up, please?"

So there were two more bodies to be taken care of and more paperwork to be done. It was late when George finally went home. The journal was still on his desk — unread.

It was Tuesday morning when Go-Ahead Rider, Elwood Lovely, and Sheriff Dooley of Cooweescoowee District rode together out to the Fletcher ranch. They were stopped at the main gate by four cowhands.

"Hold it right there," said one of the four. "No one gets through here. Mr. Fletcher's orders."

"I think you'd ought to let us through, Bub," said Dooley. "This here is Go-Ahead Rider, high sheriff of the Cherokee Nation. You know me, sheriff of Cooweescoowee District, and this here is Deputy United States Marshal Elwood Lovely. Now I don't think you boys want to buck all that authority, do you?"

"Bub," said one of the other riders, "maybe we'd ought to back off."

"No. Shut up, Little Joe," said the one called Bub. "Mr. Fletcher said no one, and he's the one who buys my beans."

"Now look here," Lovely began, but Dooley stopped him short.

"Let me talk to them," he said. "I know these boys."

Lovely heaved an exasperated sigh.

"All right," he said. "Go on."

"Bub," said Dooley, "we ain't here to start no shooting war. We don't want to fight with you boys. Hell, we don't want to fight no one. We just want to go in there and talk to Mr. Fletcher."

"And his kid," Lovely added.

A cowboy who had been quiet up until then spoke out at that.

"I knew that damn kid would cause trouble sooner or later."

"Charlie," said Bub, "just keep quiet, will you? Look, Mr. Dooley, I don't want to fight you neither. You've always treated me and the rest of the boys real fair. But you know how it is with Mr. Fletcher. If I let you through here, all four of us will be hunting jobs. You know that."

"By God," said Lovely, growing tired of the banter, "if you don't let us through, all four of you will be charged with federal crimes, and you'll wind up sitting in the federal jail at Fort Smith. You won't have to worry about a job then."

Go-Ahead Rider had kept quiet through most of this. After all, it was Dooley's district, and Dooley knew these people. And it was Lovely's case. But at last he decided that someone needed to inject a little common sense into the discussion.

"Say," he said, "why don't just one of you boys ride on down to the ranch house and tell Mr. Fletcher who it is waiting out here to see him? Reckon you could do that? That way there'd still be three of you here watching us. We'll just wait here for that one rider to bring back the word. Okay?"

The four cowboys looked at one another.

"What do you say, Bub?" asked Little Joe.

"I say you ride on in and tell Mr. Fletcher what the situation is out here. And hurry up."

"I'll do her," said Little Joe, and he whipped his cow pony around, kicked her sides, and lashed at her with his quirt. He was off like a spooked rabbit.

George assured Lee that he was all right. He'd gotten a good night's sleep, and his head felt as good as ever. Now he needed to get on down to the jail and turn Beehunter loose. George decided to keep Swim on at the National Prison for a little longer, since someone had to be there with two prisoners in two cells again, but he could only justify one deputy at the jail, and Beehunter could not speak English. And George finally recalled that he himself had been on his way to look up Councilman Peck for an interview when someone had conked him on the head. Well, he would do that this morning. He would take care of things at the office, and then go out and find Peck.

Swim was sitting up in the office and Beehunter was asleep in the next room when George walked in.

"Coffee's on," said Swim.

George poured himself a cup and sat down at his desk.

"You get any sleep last night, Delbert?" he asked.

Yeah," said Swim. "Beehunter set up most of the night."

"Well, when he wakes up," said George,

"tell him he can go on home. And tell him I said thanks. He did a good job."

"I'll tell him," said Swim. "What about me?"

"You stay here," said George. "I've got some things to do out of the office, so I need you here."

"Okay."

George finished his coffee and put his coat and hat back on. He stepped outside into the chilly air just in time to meet Mr. Downing, the principal from the seminary, coming up the walk to the jail.

"Mr. Tanner," said Downing. "Just the man I wanted to see. Do you have a minute?"

"Well, I — Yeah. Sure, Mr. Downing," said George. "Come on in."

He led the way back into the office and got a chair for the principal. They both sat down.

"Coffee?" said George.

"No, thank you," said Downing. "Mr. Tanner, you must know that the school is in a bind, due to the untimely death of Mr. Lang. There's no one to teach his classes, and we're right in the middle of the term."

"I'm sure that's true," said George, "but why come to the sheriff's office? I'd think that you'd need to go to the chief for authorization to hire a new teacher. It shouldn't be a problem: The salary's already there. The job exists."

"Oh, I have the authorization, Mr. Tanner,"

said Downing, "but a search would take too much time. Mr. Lang had a hundred students. They're all left at loose ends."

"Well, I don't understand what you want me to do about it," said George.

"I understand that you have a degree in the classics," said Downing. "From Harvard. Is that correct?"

"Well, yes, I do, but I've never used it. Besides, I already have a job."

"It's not what you were trained to do," said Downing. "There are any number of men in this country who could take over the job of deputy sheriff. You are the only classics scholar around. You're wasting your education and your talent. I might even say that you're shirking your responsibility to the next generation."

George stood up and paced over to the stove. Downing's words reminded him of an argument he'd had just recently with Rider. He picked up the coffeepot and poured himself another cup.

"Mr. Downing," he said, "I don't know what to say. When I finished my degree, when I first came back to Tahlequah, I wanted nothing more than such a position. I'd have jumped at the chance, but now . . ."

He sipped some coffee from his cup. It burned all the way down his throat.

"Can you give me a day or two to think it over?" he said. "A chance to talk with Captain Rider and with my wife?"

Downing stood up and held out his hand. George took it in his.

"Of course," said Downing. "I realize it's a big decision for you to make, and the request, I'm sure, seems rather sudden, but I hope you'll give me an answer by Friday morning, and I hope that it will be yes."

George waited a couple of minutes to allow Downing time to get well on his way. He tried to get his mind back onto business. He had a murder case on his hands, and it was the murder of a good friend. He felt a little guilty that, under such circumstances, he had allowed Downing to turn his head.

But he had just actually been offered a job teaching the classics at the Cherokee Male Seminary, a job that only a few short years ago he had coveted. It didn't help his conscience any that the job had belonged to Chris Lang, and that it would not have been offered to George had Chris not been murdered.

A part of him was puffed up that Downing had asked him, but another part wished that Downing had stayed the hell away and let him alone. He wondered what Rider would say, and he wondered what Lee would say, but most of all, he wondered, when it came right down to it, what he would say to Downing for his answer.

—18—

Five riders came fast from the Fletcher ranch house, a cloud of dust trailing behind them. When they were about halfway down the long lane that led to the gate, Rider recognized Coyne Fletcher and the cowboy called Little Joe. Elwood Lovely leaned toward Rider.

"Is one of them young Fletcher?" he asked.

"Nope," said Rider, "but that's the old man in the middle."

"Yeah," said Lovely. "I figured. Well, we'd best be ready for anything."

The deputy marshal's hand moved to his revolver.

"Aw, Elwood," said Rider, "I don't think there'll be no shooting."

"Coyne won't start nothing like that," said Dooley. "I've known the old man for years. He'll talk tough. That's all."

"Maybe so," said Lovely, "but we can't let him defy the law. We can't back down, Rider. You know that."

"It seems to me there's something somewhere in between backing down and starting a war, Elwood," said Rider. "Just take it easy."

Lovely harrumphed and moved his hand back up to his saddle horn. The five riders pulled up at the gate, the dust cloud hovering around them.

"Howdy, Mr. Fletcher," said Dooley.

"Good morning, gents," said Fletcher. "What's your business here?"

"I think you know the answer to that question, Fletcher," said Lovely. "We've come for your boy."

"Well, you ain't taking him," said Fletcher. "Boys."

Seven rifles in the hands of seven cowboys were raised and cocked almost at once, their muzzles pointed generally in the direction of the three lawmen. Lovely flinched, and his horse pranced.

"I'm a deputy United States marshal," he said.

"I know that," said Fletcher, "and I'm a Cherokee citizen, and Go-Ahead Rider there is high sheriff of the Cherokee Nation. I got more respect for his position than for yours. Even so, I ain't going to let either one of you take my boy. Not without a fight."

"You can't get away with this," said Lovely. "You stop us, and there'll be a thirty-man posse out here. You can't fight the United States."

"By the time they get here," said Coyne, "you'll be dead, and Coley'll be long gone."

"Back off, Elwood," said Rider. "Coyne, can we talk? You and me?"

Coyne Fletcher thought a moment. Then

he climbed down out of the saddle.

"Boys," he said, "keep them other two covered."

He started walking along the fence line, away from the crowd. Rider dismounted and followed him. Out of earshot, Fletcher stopped. He turned to face Rider.

"All right," he said. "What have you got to say?"

"Coyne, we don't want no trouble here. We just want to talk to Coley. That's all."

"You ain't here to arrest him?"

"No. I ain't."

"What about that deputy marshal?"

"Right now, he don't know what he wants. A white man was killed back at Tahlequah, a teacher at the seminary."

"I heard all about that. Coley didn't do it, Rider. I know my boy. He told me what happened. He found the body, got some blood on him, and got scared. That's all."

"And that's what we want to talk to him about," said Rider. "Maybe he could tell us something that would help us figure out who the killer is. Then there's the matter of him breaking into the school and stealing that exam paper."

"He put it back."

"Yeah, I know. I don't reckon that the Cherokee Nation will want to prosecute him for that, but likely he'll be kicked out of school."

Fletcher looked at the ground.

"He shouldn't have been in school anyhow. His heart wasn't in it. That was my fault. But what about the horse he stole?"

"The way I see it," said Rider, "he didn't steal no horse. He rented that animal. He just kept it longer than he said he would, and he ain't returned it and paid what he owes yet. That's all."

"Well, I don't know," said Fletcher. "I trust you, Rider. Always have. But I don't know about that damn federal lawman. It seems to me that he's just itching to get his hands on my boy."

"Elwood's all right," said Rider. "He just talks tough. Now why don't you and Coley ride on back to Tahlequah with us and straighten this whole mess out? Bring along some of your boys, if it will make you feel better."

Fletcher hesitated, deep in thought. A gunfight with the law — combined Cherokee Nation and federal law — would ruin him. He would lose everything he had worked so long and hard to build for his family. On the other hand, he was not going to stand by and see his only son arrested for murder, and maybe hung.

"Coyne," said Rider, "it's either that or make an outlaw out of your boy. Trust me on this. We'll go to my office and talk with Elwood there. Get Coley's story about finding the body. Just to verify what the

199

other boy told us. Then you and Coley can go out to the school and settle things there. Take care of the bill at the hotel, turn the horse back in and pay for it, and then you all can be on your way back home. It'll all be over. Nobody'll even get put in a cell."

"You get that deputy marshal to agree to what you just said, and I'll go along," said Fletcher. "But I want his word first."

George Tanner rode up into the yard of the fine two-story home of Councilman Peck in Tahlequah. He had already learned that Peck was there rather than at his other house in his home district of Sequoyah. He tied the reins of his mount to the ring in the hand of the small plaster cast of a uniformed black stable boy that stood in front of the porch. Then he climbed the stairs and was headed for the door, when it was opened from the inside. Ira Peck stepped out onto the porch.

"I saw you coming," he said. "Do you mind if we talk outside? I know it's cold, but my wife and children are at home. I don't want them to hear any of this."

"You know why I've come then," said George.

"Yes. I think so. I know that Mr. Lang has been murdered. It's horrible. I also heard that you have Mr. Winters locked up in jail."

"Winters is in one of our cells," said George, "but he was arrested by Elwood Lovely on a whiskey charge. We're just holding him for Deputy Marshal Lovely. The Lang case is Lovely's too, of course, though we've been helping him with the investigation."

"I see."

"Councilman, we know that you and Winters were secretly working together on behalf of the railroad interests. And we know that Chris Lang had seen you two together in Philadelphia. We also believe that either you or Mr. Winters paid Chris a visit in his office the night he was killed."

"I'll save you some trouble, Mr. Tanner," said Peck. "I went to Lang's office that night. I found the building locked, but I had seen a light in Lang's office through the window, so I went around to the window and tapped on it to get his attention. When he opened the window, I asked him to let me in. I met him back at the front door, he unlocked it, and we went to his office to talk."

"What did you talk about, Mr. Peck?"

"I asked him to keep it to himself that he had seen me and Mr. Winters together. He said that he would be happy to oblige, but that he was afraid he'd already let the cat out of the bag — he had spoken to Mr. Winters in front of you."

"That's right," said George. "He did. What else?"

"Nothing else. He was sorry if he'd caused me any problems, assured me that he would say no more, and I left."

"Did he lock the building again after you left?"

"Why, yes, I'm sure that he did. He walked with me to the front door, and I remember that he had his key out. Yes. He did."

"Thank you, Mr. Peck," said George. He turned and walked down the steps to his waiting horse.

"You're not going to arrest me?" said Peck.

"For what?" said George. "No. But I expect there'll be an investigation by the council."

"Yes," said Peck. "I'm sure you're right about that. I've already written my letter of resignation."

George looked at Peck for a moment.

"That's good," he said. He swung up into the saddle, turned his mount, and rode away.

Tommy Snail walked timidly into the office of Mr. Downing. He was so quiet that he'd been standing there for a long moment before the principal even realized he was there.

"Tommy," said Downing, registering surprise. "I didn't hear you come in. Sit down."

"Mr. Downing," said Tommy, "I just came in to tell you that I'm going home."

"But I thought that you were sick in bed. You look to me like you should still be in bed. How are you feeling?"

"I'm all right," said Tommy. He was

looking at the floor.

"Are you sure? You don't look all right to me. Come on. Why don't we go back up to bed, and you rest until you get better."

"No," said Tommy, almost shouting. He took a couple of steps backward, away from Downing, who had come out from behind his desk. Downing stopped, startled.

"Tommy," he said. "What's the matter?"

"Nothing. I just want to go home. That's all."

Downing sat on the edge of his desk.

"If you insist on going home, I can't stop you," he said. "I won't even try. But if something's wrong, I need to know about it."

He paused, hoping for something from Tommy, but Tommy just stared at the floor.

"How will you get home?" asked Downing.

"Walk."

"It's a long way," said Downing. "It's cold out there. I'm afraid you'll just get worse. Why don't you —"

"I'm not going back up there," said Tommy.

"All right," said Downing, giving up. "Let me get my coat on. I'll get the buggy and drive you home."

Back at the office, George told Delbert Swim to go on home and get some rest.

"I'll stay here until Rider gets back," he said. "If we still need you, we'll let you know."

"Okay, George," said Swim. He picked up his hat and coat and started for the door. "I'll be at home."

"Thanks, Delbert," said George. He sat down at his desk and picked up Lang's journal. He opened it and read the first page. It had to do with Lang's initial interview with Peck. George put the book down, still opened to that first page. He stared at it without seeing. He was thinking of Chris. This journal, he thought, must have been started as a chronicle of Chris's new adventure in the Cherokee Nation.

What an adventure it had turned out to be. A young man, just starting his career. A good man, doing good work. Cut down. Murdered. And for what? Why had he been killed? Why? George pushed the journal aside and began to write on a notepad.

1. Because he whipped Willit Barnes?
2. Because he had seen Peck and Winters together?
3. Because he caught Coley Fletcher stealing the exam?
4. Something else? What?

He stared at his list. He could not believe that Willit Barnes had done the deed, especially not now that Willit had come in and confessed to the more recent murder of his own father. If Willit had killed Lang, why not admit that too? He could only hang once.

On the other hand, what if Willit managed to get off easy for the killing of his father? He knew that he had the sympathy of several lawmen who had seen the results of the recent beating old man Barnes had given him. He might get off, and no one would suspect him of the other killing precisely because he had already confessed to this one. George didn't really think Willit had murdered Lang, but he had to admit that it was still a possibility.

What about Peck and Winters then? Peck admitted having gone to Lang's office, and the tale he told coincided with the physical evidence George and Rider had discovered at the scene of the crime. The footprints went where Peck said he had gone, and George recalled that earlier he and Rider and Lovely had all agreed that if they were to find out who Lang's shoe-wearing visitor was, they would have the killer.

But something about Peck's forthright attitude made George believe that the man was not guilty. True, Peck was practiced in deceit, and seeing the law closing in on him, he could have been putting on an act for George. But George didn't think so. He could much more easily suspect Winters of murder than Peck.

Could Winters have also paid a visit to Lang's office that night? It seemed that everyone else had. But if Peck had gone to see Lang, it was unlikely that Winters would also have done so. The two men had undoubtedly discussed their mutual problem and had decided that Peck would deal with it.

Then there was Coley Fletcher. Coley had been drinking. He had broken into Lang's office to steal an exam in order to copy it for the purpose of cheating. He had copied it, then gone back and broken in a second time to replace it. He had been at the scene, and he had been there with the body. He had blood on his hands and on his clothes.

The strongest evidence pointed at Coley, yet it was not totally convincing. First of all the motive — getting caught at cheating on an exam — didn't seem strong enough for murder. And then the position of the body and the location of Coley's footprints on the office floor didn't fit together in the right way.

On the one hand, George couldn't quite bring himself to believe that any one of his four suspects was actually the murderer. On the other, he couldn't quite eliminate any of them either. That left him with number four: "Something else? What?" And who, he asked himself, and why?

—19—

It was late in the day when Go-Ahead Rider, accompanied by Elwood Lovely, Coyne Fletcher, and Coley Fletcher, arrived back in Tahlequah. Coley was leading the rented horse. They rode past the National Hotel and on down Muskogee Avenue until they were just about even with the National Prison, a block to their left. Rider stopped the small party there. Lovely glanced down toward the jail on Water Street, wondering just what the hell Rider was up to.

"Coyne," Rider said, "I think you and Coley have got just about enough time left to get that horse turned in. Then I suggest that you get yourselves a room back down at the hotel. There might be some settling up to do there too. Then get a good night's rest and come on by the office in the morning. Me and Elwood'll both be there."

Coyne gave Rider a nod.

"We'll be there," he said. "Have the coffee on."

As the Fletchers moved south down Muskogee Avenue toward the stable where Coley had rented the horses, Lovely gave Rider a hard look.

"Rider," he said, "what the hell are you doing with my prisoners?"

"Did you put them under arrest, Elwood?" asked Rider, feigning surprise. "I must have missed that."

"Well, I never actually —"

"It's all right, Elwood," said Rider. "They'll be by in the morning, just like Coyne said. Now, let's you and me go on over to the office and get a cup of coffee. Get the chill out of our bones."

He turned his horse toward the jail, and Lovely followed. They rode the animals into the sheriff's barn behind the prison and put them away for the night, then walked over to the jail. George stood up when they came into the office. He knew they'd had a long and cold ride.

"Coffee?" he said.

"You bet," said Rider, shedding his hat and coat.

"Yeah," said Lovely. "Thanks."

He was still feeling grumpy about Rider's casual treatment of the Fletchers. George handed him a cup of hot coffee, and Lovely took it to the straight chair that sat against the wall. Rider got his cup and went behind his desk. He put the cup down on the desktop, pulled the Colts out of his waistband and laid one on each side of the cup, then sat down.

"You find Coley Fletcher?" asked George.

"Him and his daddy are down at the hotel," said Rider. "They'll drop by in the morning."

"Rider," said Lovely, "by rights that Fletcher boy ought to be my prisoner. The old man too. Hell, we ought to have them both in a cell right now."

"What're you going to arrest them for, Elwood?" asked Rider. "What charge?"

"Well, hell, suspicion of murder on the kid. What else?"

"Then you going to arrest Willit Barnes and Winters too, on the same charge?"

"And Councilman Peck?" added George.

"You keep out of this, Tanner," said Lovely, and back to Rider, he pointed out, "I *have* arrested Winters."

"On a whiskey charge," said Rider. "Elwood, I know this is your case, but me and George here, we want it cleared up as bad as you do. Maybe worse. But now, you tell me, do you really think that Fletcher boy did that killing?"

"Well, hell," said Lovely, "I don't know. But we know he was there. And he had blood on him. He also had a reason. Likely he got caught breaking in. My boss would say that's enough to arrest him on. It might even be enough to convict him and hang him."

"And he might not be guilty," said Rider, "and the real killer would still be running around loose. I know you don't want that."

"No," grumbled Lovely. He sipped at the hot coffee. It felt good after the long cold ride, and he could feel himself softening up a little from the inside. Actually, he knew that Rider was right. Rider was nearly always right, and sometimes that aggravated Lovely just a bit.

He had come to Tahlequah to pick up a prisoner, and he had intended to turn right around and return to Muskogee that same day. Then this murder had been dropped in his lap. Lovely didn't like this kind of work. He liked being handed a warrant and told to go out and get his man. He was no good at this investigating, and he knew it. But Rider was good at it, and Tanner was too, and getting better all the time. Lovely knew that Rider was right, so he wasn't really angry at him. He was just frustrated. He wanted to arrest someone.

"I don't think you want to arrest no one till you know for sure," said Rider. Lovely almost flinched. It was as if Rider had read his mind. He hadn't, of course; he had just picked up the conversation again. "Let's just all of us get a good night's sleep and then we'll talk to the boy in the morning," Rider concluded.

Lovely finished off the coffee in his cup. He stood up and carried the cup over to the stove and put it down, then pulled his coat together in front and put his hat back on, snugging it down tight on his head.

"Well, hell, I'm going to the hotel," he said. "At least I'll be sleeping in the same damn building with them. I'm going to catch hell for my expenses on this trip."

"You're welcome to bed down here," said Rider.

"Nah, it's too late today anyhow," said Lovely. "They're going to charge me for that room for tonight whether I show up or not. I'll see you in the morning."

After Lovely had shut the outside door, George looked over at Rider.

"He seemed just a little bit upset," he said.

"He'll be all right."

"That's why I didn't tell the other story while he was here."

"What story?"

"About the jailbreak and the two killings."

Rider leaned forward, his elbows on his desktop.

"Well, maybe you better tell me," he said.

George gave Rider the details about the lump on his head, the escape of Winters and Avery, and Beehunter's pursuit of the escapees and their accomplice, Harkey. He told him how Beehunter had come back to Tahlequah with a battered and dejected Winters and the bodies of the other two.

"Winters admitted everything," he added. "He's lost his pomposity. I think the whole

211

thing scared him half to death. Avery killed Harkey on the road when Harkey's horse went lame. Beehunter killed Avery, resisting arrest."

"The man was a fool to put up a fight against Beehunter," said Rider. "That was the right thing to do, George, sending Beehunter out."

"You can credit Exie with that," said George. "So anyhow, Winters can now be charged with jailbreak in addition to the whiskey charge," he added. "Maybe even accessory to a murder."

"And assaulting an officer of the law," added Rider. "Resisting arrest. Just depends on how far Elwood wants to take it. Well, it's just as well you waited to tell it. I don't know if old Elwood could have stood to hear that tale tonight; morning will be soon enough. You've had a couple of rough days, George. Why don't you go on home to Lee and the baby. I'll take care of things here."

"You sure?"

"I'm sure."

"We got two prisoners again."

"Two?"

"Oh, yeah. Willit Barnes is in a cell. He killed his daddy."

Rider heaved a sigh and leaned his head heavily in his hands.

"I can't say I'm surprised," he said. "Not really. I was afraid something like that would

212

happen. You know, George, it's a damn shame that even if we know about it, we can't do nothing about a bad situation until somebody kills someone."

"Yeah," said George, standing up. "How about I go by Delbert Swim's house on my way home and send him on down here?"

"Yeah," said Rider. "That's a good idea. I'll stay here and wait for him."

"Okay."

George got his hat and coat and started out the door. He paused, turned, and spoke again.

"Rider?"

"Yeah?"

"Mr. Downing, the principal out at the seminary, asked me to take over for Chris."

"You mean teaching?"

"Yeah."

"He talking about a job?"

"Yeah. Chris's job. There's students without a teacher. Their classes have just stopped."

"That's a full-time job, George," said Rider. "You'd have to quit here."

"Yes, I would."

"You going to do it?"

"Well, I want to talk to you about it," said George.

Rider leaned back in his chair and put his feet up on his desk.

"Okay," he said. "Let's talk in the morning."

"Good night, Rider. I'll send Delbert along right away."

"Good night, George," said Rider.

He waited until he knew that George was gone, and then he got up and went to find Willit Barnes in his cell. He figured the boy might want someone to talk to.

"I told Rider tonight about Mr. Downing offering me Chris's job," George said to Lee. He had just pulled off his boots and was leaning back in an easy chair. Lee was in a rocker, holding little Rider on her shoulder.

"The way you told it to me, it was more than an offer," she said. "It was more like he begged you to take the position."

"Well . . ."

"What did Rider say?"

"He said let's talk about it tomorrow."

"You have to take it, George," said Lee. "You're not thinking of turning it down, are you?"

"It's Rider I'm thinking about," said George. "He gave me a job when I needed one, gave me a place to stay until I could get something for myself. He and Exie practically took me in like one of their family."

"I know that. Rider's a good friend, and he'll always be a good friend, but you're not tied to him professionally, George. He'd tell you that himself. This position is what you're trained for. It's what you've always wanted."

"I know. But I never wanted to get it as a result of the death of a friend."

"Oh, George."

She could tell that the decision was a difficult, almost painful one for George to make. She knew how much his association with Go-Ahead Rider meant to him, and she knew that he was thinking that it would be disloyal of him to quit Rider. And from his last statement, she knew that he was also feeling some guilt at the possibility of profiting from the death of a friend.

But it was not a situation of his making, and he had not sought the position — Mr. Downing had come to him. She wanted him to accept the job. It was his interest in the classics that had first brought them together. He was a good scholar, and she knew that he would make a good teacher.

And — although she would keep this to herself, and would not use it to try to force him to make what she knew was the right decision — she would be much more comfortable as the wife of a teacher than she was as the wife of a lawman.

As the wife of a deputy sheriff, she had to worry each day about her husband's safety. If he were to become a teacher, that worry would be eliminated from her life. She was aware of the irony, given the fate of poor Chris Lang. Still, she knew, the notion was a valid one. The murder of Chris Lang was not typical. The death of a lawman in the line of duty was all too common.

"I'm all right," said George. "I'll talk it over with Rider in the morning, and I'll go talk to Mr. Downing again. I don't even know what the salary is."

"But I'm not sleepy," Buster whined, speaking in Cherokee.

"It's time for you to go to bed," said Exie, also in Cherokee. "You have to get up and go to school in the morning."

"Go on now," said Rider. "I'll come home early tomorrow, and we'll have plenty of time together."

"All of us?" asked Tootie.

"Yes," said Rider. "All of us. Go on now."

Mumbling to each other, the kids went to bed. Rider puffed at his corncob pipe.

"*Kawi jaduli?*" asked Exie.

"One more cup," he said. "Then I'm going to bed. It's been a long two days, and I have to get at it early again in the morning."

Exie got his cup and refilled it. She handed it to him.

"*Wado,*" he said.

She sat down and looked at him for a moment. She could tell he was troubled.

"You're worrying about something," she said. "You should relax and think about it tomorrow."

"Yes," he said. "You're right."

He sipped some coffee, put the cup down, and leaned back in his chair.

"Exie," he said.

"Yes?"

"I'm going to have to hire a new deputy."

"What?"

"I'm going to lose George. They want him at the seminary."

"Will he go there, do you think?"

"George has been a good deputy," said Rider. "I've been able to rely on him a lot. He learns fast. He's smart. But I'm going to have to let him go. He's been to college, and he has that degree. He's trained for the job at the seminary, and it's what he meant to do all along."

"So who will you hire to replace Jaji?"

"I don't think I *can* replace him," said Rider. "He's been a good one." He puffed at his pipe. It went out, and he laid it aside. "I think I'll have to hire Delbert Swim — if he wants the job. I'm not sure that Delbert wants to work steadily. I'd rather have Beehunter, but I think the judge would balk at that. We've gotten to the point where one has to speak English to work for the Cherokee Nation."

The irony of Rider's last statement was poignant, the words having been spoken in the Cherokee language.

—20—

The interview with the Fletchers went about as Rider had expected, even, to a certain extent, predicted, although Elwood Lovely's calm reaction was surprising. He accepted it all, or at least seemed to, with a modicum of grace, and finally the Fletchers got up to leave the office. Coyne Fletcher vigorously pumped Rider's hand and thanked him profusely for all his help and understanding.

They had, he said, already settled with Sim at the hotel and with Curly at the stable, leaving those two worthy gentlemen more than satisfied, and before heading out of Tahlequah, they were going to stop by the seminary, where Coley would confess his crimes and resign from his life as a student with as much dignity as possible, under the circumstances.

"From now on," said Coyne Fletcher, "Coley will be my right hand. He's going to be the best damn rancher you ever saw."

"He'll have a ways to go," said Rider, "to catch up with you."

"You're right, Sheriff," said Coley, "but I'm going to try. It's all I ever wanted."

"Good luck to you, son," said Rider.

The two Fletchers left the building, and Rider went to the stove to refill his cup.

"We're still basically just taking the Fletcher kid's word for it," said Lovely. "Sometimes I think you're just too damn soft."

"Well, the evidence at the scene of the crime seems to back his story up pretty well," said Rider. "We're just going to have to think this whole thing through again, all the way from the beginning."

"Shit," said Lovely. "What you mean is that we ain't got nowhere, and we're starting all over."

"Not exactly," said Rider. "Sometimes you have to clear a whole bunch of stuff out of your way before you can start to get at the truth. That's all. But first, we got another matter to deal with here."

"What's that?" asked Lovely.

"Old George here has been offered another job."

"Oh, well," said George, "that can wait, Rider. I —"

"The way I hear it," said Rider, "there's a whole bunch of students out there at the seminary who can't afford to wait. It's right smack in the middle of their term, and they ain't got a teacher. I think maybe you'd ought to get on out there, George."

"What? Right now?"

"Ain't no sense in putting it off, is there?"

"But I can't just walk out of here," said George, "just like that. Not when we've got so much to do here. I wouldn't feel right about that."

"George," said Rider, "we've cleared up a whole bunch of the questions we had. Now me and Elwood are just going to go all the way back to the beginning and see what we can come up with. You know, officially, you and me ain't busy at all — this murder ain't our case."

"I know that, Rider, but, well, it just doesn't seem like the right time."

"The time never does seem right, George. Things happen when they happen." Rider took out his pipe and tobacco and started to fill the bowl. "Tell you what," he said. "Suppose I was to just write you up as being on a . . . what do you call it? A leave of absence. How would that be?"

"A leave of absence?" said George.

"Yeah. You know. That way, if for any reason the other thing don't work out, you can always come back. Your job here will be waiting for you."

"You can't hold it open forever," said George.

"Well," said Rider, striking a match on the edge of his desktop, "how long would I need to hold it for? Till the end of the school year? That be long enough?"

"Sure, but — well, you'll have to hire another deputy, a temporary replacement."

Rider puffed on his pipe to get it going, and a cloud of smoke rose around his head.

"Yeah," he said. "I thought about that."

"Who will you get?"

"What do you say to old Delbert Swim? You think he could handle it?"

George wanted to say, Delbert can't do all the things I do. He wanted to say, how can you think of replacing me with Delbert? And he wanted to ask how Rider could even begin to think of trying to get along without him. But he didn't say any of those things.

"Beehunter's a better man," he said.

"You're right there. Ain't no one better than Beehunter," Rider agreed. "Only thing is, he can't talk English. Hell, George, even our chief can't talk Cherokee. You know that. I couldn't leave Beehunter here alone, and I couldn't send him over to the capitol to take care of any business there. No. I wish it was different, but I'm afraid it's going to have to be Delbert. Unless you got someone else in mind."

"No. I don't. I guess you're right about all that," said George. He admitted to himself that he was a little hurt that Rider didn't consider him to be irreplaceable and was seriously contemplating filling his slot with Delbert Swim. But he couldn't think of anything to say that wouldn't sound pompous and arrogant.

"Well then, why don't you do me one last chore before you take off on your leave," said Rider. "Why don't you, on your way from here over to the seminary, why don't you just stop by old Delbert's place and ask him to come on over here to see me. Would you do that? You don't have to tell him what it's all about. Just ask him to come over and see me."

"Sure," said George. He stood up, hesitant, and then he unbuckled his gun belt. He was embarrassed. He felt like he was being stripped or being drummed out of the military or something. No. It was worse than that: He felt like he was being cut out of the life of Go-Ahead Rider.

He crossed the room and laid the gun and belt on the desk in front of Rider. He stood there for a moment in silence, reached up and unfastened the badge from his shirtfront, and dropped it on the desk beside the gun. "Sure," he added. "I'll do that."

Then he turned and walked to the door, picking up his hat and coat along the way. Just as he was about to go out, Rider spoke again.

"George," he said, "go on and take a horse out of the barn. It'd be a long walk out there to the school. You can bring him back later. No hurry."

"Thanks," said George, and he went on out, shutting the door behind himself. He felt like he had just shut the door on a major portion of his life, one that he was not at all sure he wanted to leave behind.

"This is kind of a bad time to be letting a good man go, ain't it, Rider?" said Lovely.

"Good a time as any," said Rider. "Besides, this murder case ain't mine anyhow. Right?"

Grumbling, Lovely stood up and paced over to the stove. He picked up a cup in his left hand and the coffeepot in his right.

"Yeah," he said. "That's right. It's mine. If you want to back off of it, you got every right. Hell, you don't owe me nothing. You ain't obligated. All right if I have some coffee?"

"Sure," said Rider. "Have a cup."

"You want me to pay for it?"

"No," said Rider, "I'll buy."

He calmly puffed his pipe and watched as Lovely poured himself some coffee, then walked back over to the chair which stood against the wall to sit and sulk.

"You know," said Rider, looking thoughtful, "old George will be working every day right out there where that killing took place. He'll be sitting in the same office Lang sat in, seeing the same people every day that Lang saw. It wouldn't surprise me a little bit if he was to come up with some new ideas on the case."

Lovely leaned forward in his chair and gave Rider a sideways look.

"You sly old son of a bitch," he said. "I might have knowed you was up to something."

"I ain't up to nothing, Elwood. George has a college education. In the classics. He belongs out there. That's all. If he was to come up with something that would help us out while he's teaching, why, that's just extra."

"Sure, Rider," said Lovely. "Sure."

And he was smiling for the first time in three days. But no one had yet told him about the jailbreak.

Holding his hat politely in front of his belt buckle, George stepped into the open doorway of the principal's office at the seminary. Downing was busy with some paperwork, hunkered over his desk with his head down. George cleared his throat to get Downing's attention.

"Mr. Downing," he said.

Downing looked up. When he saw who it was, he got quickly up out of his chair and hurried around the desk, his hand reaching out eagerly. George shook his hand.

"Mr. Tanner," said Downing, a wide and happy smile on his face, "come in. Come in." With a sweep of his arm, he indicated a chair. "Sit down," he said. "Welcome."

George sat down in the chair, his hat placed awkwardly on his knees, while Downing perched himself casually on a corner of his desktop.

"Well," said Downing, "have you thought it over? My offer of a job. Have you considered it?"

"Yes, I have," said George. "And I came over here today to tell you that I'll accept that position. That is, if you still want me for it."

"Wonderful," said Downing, standing up and reaching again for George's hand. "That's great. Of course I still want you. I can't tell you what a load this takes off my mind. Welcome. Welcome to the faculty, Mr. Tanner."

Downing gave George's hand such a vigorous shaking that George's hat fell off his knees onto the floor. He got his hand back and reached down to pick up his hat.

"Thank you, sir," he said. "I'll finish out the school year for you at least, and then we can each see what we think about . . . well, about the future. Captain Rider was good enough to put me on a leave of absence until then."

"That sounds reasonable, Mr. Tanner," said Downing. "I'm sure that by then you'll have decided to stay on here with us. You'll love the work, and you'll become very attached to your students as well. I'm sure of it. Er, when do you want to start?"

"If it's all right with you, I'd like to go right now down to Chris — to Mr. Lang's office and look over his notes and see where he was with the different classes. And I need to look over his schedule. Then, well, I'd like to get started first thing in the morning."

"Wonderful," said Downing. "I'd like nothing better than that, and I'm sure the students feel the same way."

Downing went back around to the business side of his desk and sat down. He fumbled for a moment with some papers, then held a sheet out toward George.

"Here's a copy of your class schedule," he said. "I think we won't assign you any extra duties for the duration of this term. You'll want to know your salary, I would imagine, and perhaps a few other details about the job. Then I'll give you a key, and you can go right on down there and move into the office. It's yours."

George unlocked the office door and stepped inside. He suddenly felt terribly self-conscious. When he had first gone to work for Captain Go-Ahead Rider — the Cherokee Civil War hero, then sheriff of Tahlequah District, now high sheriff of the Cherokee Nation — George had bought himself some new clothes. He had imitated Rider's dress, and had stepped completely into the role of a law enforcement officer of the Cherokee Nation.

Now, stepping into the office and the role of a teacher at the Cherokee Male Seminary, he felt completely out of place. He remembered the day he returned from college. He had ridden into Tahlequah on the stage from Muskogee, following a long and tiring railroad trip. He had disembarked on Muskogee Avenue in the middle of a busy day, during a council meeting. The first thing he'd seen was the new two-story, red brick capitol.

He remembered that he had come home full of high hopes and ambition with his new diploma from Harvard University in his pocket. Had someone offered him a job at the seminary at that time, he would have accepted it without question. In fact, he'd had plans of applying for just such a position.

But a gunfight had erupted at the north end of town right then, and before George had known what was happening, Rider had come along and deputized him. In the Cherokee Nation, the sheriff had that authority, and if the citizen so chosen refused to serve, he could be fined. When the crisis was over, Rider had made George the offer of a full-time job, and George, overwhelmed by the reputation and the presence of Go-Ahead Rider, had accepted.

Now, standing in the former office of Chris Lang, George felt a multitude of emotions. He felt out of place, and he felt as if he had just walked out on Rider — and at a crucial time, a time when Rider especially needed help. But the case was a federal case, and after all, it had been Rider who had told George to go ahead and make the move, who had, in fact, practically shoved him out of the office.

He realized also that he had now been chasing criminals, breaking up fights, and jailing drunks for so long that he actually had doubts about his abilities to do anything else — especially to take on a teaching job and perform satisfactorily at it. The youthful cockiness that he had brought home with him from Harvard along with his fresh diploma was gone.

And finally there was the other thing. The last time he had walked into this office, Chris Lang had been lying dead right there on the floor. And the feeling that he was about to profit from the death of his friend added to the feeling of guilt and uncertainty which already crowded his troubled mind.

He looked behind himself and was glad to see no one standing behind him in the hallway. He pulled the door shut, hung his hat on a peg on the wall, and shrugged out of his coat, then hung it on a peg beside the hat and walked over to the desk.

Everything was in neat stacks, and he recalled that Lee and Exie had taken the time to go through Chris's things, both here in the office and at his home. He was glad they had done that, and he was glad too for Lee's education and experience as a schoolteacher. Confident that she had been able to get the right papers in the right stacks, even those written in Latin or in Greek, he moved behind the desk and sat down.

—21—

George walked out of his last class of the day with a tremendous sense of relief. He had completed his first day on his new job. It was over and done, and he had survived it. No, he had done more than that — he had performed remarkably well. He was proud of himself. It had all come back to him, as if he had never left the academic world. And he had really enjoyed it. It was, after all, he reminded himself, his first career choice, his first love.

The students were mostly good students, it seemed, serious and eager to learn, and George felt a sense of importance in the role he was just beginning to play in their young lives. Some of them would go on to become doctors and lawyers. Some would be the leaders of the Cherokee Nation, and he would have had a part in the formation of their lives. It was important work, probably more important, he told himself, than throwing drunks in jail.

He put his books and papers from the last class down on the desk and straightened himself up. He adjusted his vest and buttoned his jacket. Knowing that a change of costume would help him get into his new role, he was wearing a gray three-piece suit and flat shoes. And he had walked to school wearing a bowler on his head.

His workday was done, but he had a question he wanted to ask Mr. Downing, so, having adjusted his clothing, he walked down the hall to the principal's office.

"Mr. Tanner," said Downing, his smile wide, "how did your first day go?"

"It went very well, Mr. Downing," said George. "Thank you. Surprisingly well, as a matter of fact."

"I'm glad," said Downing, "but I have to tell you that I'm not surprised. I knew you'd do well, and I knew you'd like it. Do you have everything you need?"

"Oh, yes," said George. "Everything's fine. I did notice that Tommy Snail wasn't in class. Do you know if he's still upstairs, sick in bed?"

"Oh, no," said Downing, "he's not. He's gone home. In fact, I drove him home myself. I should have informed you, but with everything that's been happening around here, it just slipped my mind."

"He went home?" said George.

"Yes. I tried to talk him out of it. He didn't look well to me. I told him that I thought he should stay in bed, but he insisted on going home. He said he'd walk if he had to."

"He would certainly have been better off staying here," said George.

"He told me that he simply would not go back upstairs," said Downing.

"That's strange," said George. "He's been living here, hasn't he?"

"Yes. Just going home on weekends."

"*Some* weekends."

"Yes," said Downing. "I know what you're thinking about. I had a long talk with Coley Fletcher and his father yesterday. Coley won't be coming back to classes."

"I'm not surprised," said George, "but Tommy . . . Had he been having any problems at school?"

"None that I'm aware of," said Downing. "His grades are all excellent, and he seemed to get on well with everyone around him. I thought he was quite well-adjusted and quite happy here with us. That's why I was so surprised when he came in here and insisted on going home."

"Well, thank you, Mr. Downing," said George. "I know you have work to do. I won't take any more of your time."

"Oh, don't hesitate," said Downing. "Stop by anytime. If there's anything I can do to help, let me know."

George went back to his office and sat down. He stared at the desktop, wondering about Tommy Snail, and wondering just why he was so puzzled by Tommy's actions. He couldn't quite put a finger on it, but there was something about Tommy's insistence on going home that was bothering George. There had to be more to the story. There just had to be.

Rider heard the sounds of a buggy driving up in front of the prison. He moved over to the window to look out onto the road. A one-horse buggy had just stopped, and a man in a gray business suit and a bowler was stepping out. Rider watched as the man turned to walk toward the prison's front door. It was George Tanner.

"Look a-here, Delbert," said Rider.

Delbert Swim got up from behind the little desk that had so recently belonged to George and stepped over to Rider's side at the window. His eyes opened wide at the sight of the man approaching the steps.

"George?" he said.

Rider smiled.

"Yeah. That's our George," he said. He walked to the office door and opened it just as George was about to reach for the handle. "Come right in, Mr. Tanner," he said, stepping aside and making a sweeping gesture with his arm. "What can we do for you?"

George stepped in and took the bowler off his head. He held it clumsily, and his face flushed slightly.

"Oh, I'm just on my way home," he said.

"Thought I'd stop by and say hello. See how things're going. You see my new rig out there?"

"You buy that?" asked Rider.

"Sure did. Right after school today. Just now. I went down to the bank and got the money, then went on down to the livery and made the deal with Curly. Oh. Your horse is back in the barn."

"I know," said Rider. "I was out there this morning and seen him."

"That's a good-looking rig there, George," said Swim.

"Thank you, Delbert," said George. "I got a good horse with it too."

"Horse?" said Swim. "What horse? Oh. You're talking about that rig outside. Hell. I meant that new outfit you're wearing."

Swim laughed at his joke, and Rider chuckled. George was embarrassed, but he took it as well as he could.

"I couldn't very well go teach Latin and Greek to school kids looking like I did, could I? They'd think I was coming to put them in jail."

"Sit down, George," said Rider, starting to get up from his chair. "You want some coffee?"

"Yeah," said George. "That's all right, I can get it — I haven't been gone *that* long. And I *am* just on leave. Right?"

"That's right," said Rider.

"Don't start treating me like a guest around here all of a sudden. Not yet."

"Hell," said Rider, easing back down in his chair. "Get your own coffee then."

George hung his bowler on one of the wall pegs by the door, then went to the stove to pour himself some coffee. He moved on over to the chair against the wall, the one where Lovely usually sat. That made him conscious of the deputy marshal's absence.

"Where's Elwood?" he asked.

"He went out to get himself a beefsteak," said Rider. "That's what he said. Right after I told him about the jailbreak and how Beehunter killed old Avery."

"How did he take *that* news?" asked George.

"That was all he said — he was going out for a beefsteak."

"George," said Swim, standing up. "Come on over here. I feel funny sitting in your chair with you here."

"That's your chair now, Delbert," said George, "at least until the school year's done. Go on. Sit down. You're making me nervous."

Swim sat back down at the small desk, but he didn't look very comfortable there.

"So how'd it go at the school today?" Rider asked.

"Just fine," said George. "Real smooth. I was able to pick the classes right up and get them moving again. I have to admit, I really enjoyed myself. You know, it's what I always wanted, or at least was before you gave me this job."

"That's good, George," said Rider. "I bet you'll do them a real good job."

"Well, how are you doing?" George asked. "You and Elwood, I mean. Any progress?"

"We've just only had one day without you here, George," said Rider. "I hope you ain't expecting too much in that short time."

"No, I just —"

"We talked it around some more," Rider continued. "That's about all we could do. We did kind of come up with an interesting notion."

"Oh? What's that?"

"Well, if we read the evidence right, and if we're right about all of our original suspects, then it seems to me that there's only one thing for it. Whoever killed Chris Lang was in the building all the time. Either that, or it could've been someone else who had a key to the building."

"Rider," said George, "what you're saying is that it was someone on the staff of the seminary."

"Sounds that way, don't it?" said Rider. "Think it through. All the sign at the scene of the crime indicates that two people went up to the office window. One of them climbed through. The other'n went around to the front door and was let in."

"Coley Fletcher was the one who went through the window," said George. "He was wearing boots. Tommy Snail told us that Coley went through the window, and Coley himself finally admitted it."

"But he says that he didn't do it, and I believe him," said Rider, "partly because of the footprints he left on the office floor and the position of the body. And no one else went through the window, not so far as we can tell."

"And besides all that, it's unlikely that someone could have come through the window and gotten around behind Chris, with Chris facing into the room," said George. "So the killer did not come in through the window. And the shoe prints that went around to the front door belonged to Councilman Peck. He admitted to me that he visited Chris that night in the office."

"He tapped on the window and got Chris to go meet him at the front door and let him in," said Rider. "They went to the office and had a talk, then went together back to the front door."

"Chris let him out and locked the door behind him," said George. "That's what Peck said. Of course, Peck could have done it, then put out the light, and taken Chris's key to lock the door after he left. That's the way we had it figured in the first place."

"That's awful meticulous, though, ain't it?" said Rider. "Is that the right word? 'Meticulous'?"

"What do you mean?" said George.

"Well, if someone's just committed a murder, he'd likely be thinking of getting away from the scene, not locking the door."

"But if it was done by somebody inside," said George, "what happened to Chris's key?"

"I don't know." Rider shrugged. "Maybe the killer took it to throw us off."

"Could be," said George. "But now you've got this new killer being awful" — he looked over at Rider — "meticulous."

"If he was inside, he wasn't thinking about getting away — he was thinking about covering his tracks."

"All right," said George. "Maybe."

"Our only other suspects were Winters and poor ol' Willit Barnes," said Rider. "I can't believe it was Winters, for two reasons. First off, there's no evidence of a third party getting into the building that night, and second, there wasn't no reason for Winters to see Lang when Peck had already done it for the both of them."

"Yeah, and there never was really any evidence against Willit," George added. "We only questioned him in the first place because he had fought with Chris."

Rider leaned back in his chair and put his feet up on the desk.

"So?" he said.

George heaved a long sigh of resignation.

"So if someone else got into the building, it was someone with a key," he said. "If no one else got into the building, then someone who was already there has to be the killer."

"You got it, George," said Rider. "You got it."

Delbert Swim stood up and moved to the stove. He poured himself some coffee.

"You two just about made my head swim with all that," he said. "Boy. I don't know how you do it."

"It ain't that hard, Delbert," said Rider. "If you'd have been with us from the beginning, you'd be right along with us now."

"I don't know," said Swim, shaking his head slowly.

"So what do we do now, Rider?" said George.

"You go on with your new job," said Rider. "Me and ol' Elwood, we'll press on with this inquiry. 'Course, it's Elwood's decision, not mine. If any one of us here was to do anything on our own, it'd be outside the law. But what I'll suggest to Elwood is that we start in interviewing everyone on the staff at the seminary. Starting with Downing."

"Yeah," said George. "That's about all you can do, isn't it?" He stood up and took his cup back over to the stove. "Well," he said, "I'd better be going along. I have some work to do for tomorrow's classes, and, uh, Lee hasn't seen the new rig yet. The one outside, I mean."

Swim laughed.

"Yeah," said Rider, standing up and moving around the desk to take George by the arm. "You'd best be getting on home then."

"She'll be wanting to take a ride in that new buggy," said Swim.

"You might be right about that," said George as he walked over to get his bowler. "Well, I'll be seeing you."

"Oh, George," said Rider. "Just a minute. Here's a couple of things you left here. You might want them."

Out of a desk drawer, he picked up the journal and the notepad that Lee had brought from Lang's house, and held them out toward George.

"Oh yeah," said George, taking them from Rider. "Thanks. I forgot all about them. Lee told me to read this. I'd better do it tonight."

—22—

"These are some of the most — important — laws of Solon. He — caused the Athenians to swear to keep his laws for — one hundred years, but after an — absence — of ten years in — Egypt — he found that his laws were being ignored. He went to — Cyprus and helped to build the city of Soli. He died at the age of — eighty years."

George was standing in front of the class listening to a young half-breed reading aloud from the Latin text of Plutarch's *Life of Solon*. The young man finished the paragraph, the last in the story, and looked up tentatively at George.

"That was good, Stanley," George said. "Thank you. Now, let's forget about the Latin just for now and think about the ideas in the text we've just read. Solon was a lawmaker. Think about the laws he wrote and compare them with the laws we live under here in the Cherokee Nation. How would we feel about living under the laws of Solon?"

Stanley raised his hand.

"Yes, Stanley," said George.

"Well, sir," said Stanley, "I think that some of them would be all right, but other ones would be pretty bad."

"Can you give us an example?"

"Well, the law that said debts should be forgiven would make a lot of people mad," said Stanley. "If you owed someone some money, you wouldn't have to pay him back."

"That's right," said George. "That one even made people mad at Solon during his own lifetime, didn't it?"

"Yes, sir."

"Good. What else?"

Another hand shot up toward the back of the room, and George acknowledged it.

"Whenever he repealed the laws of that guy Draco," said the young man, "that was pretty good. Before that they were executing people for everything — stealing apples and being idle and such."

"Yes," said George. "I think we'd all agree with the repeal of the Draconian laws, wouldn't we?"

"Yeah," said another young man, "but what about that law against speaking ill of the dead?"

"What about it?" said George.

"Well, that's not so good, is it? I mean, maybe it's not nice to say bad things about someone after he's dead, but I don't think someone ought to go to jail for doing it. Or have to pay a fine or anything."

"No. We probably wouldn't put up with that, would we?" said George. Just then, through the open door, he noticed Rider and Lovely walking down the hall. He knew what they were up to. Lovely had taken Rider's suggestion that they interview everyone at the school. George wanted to talk to Rider and Lovely. He had some new information, and he wanted to pass it along to them. He also wanted to be in on the interviews, for he had questions of his own that he wanted to ask.

Suddenly the time seemed to pass slowly, and the rest of the class hour dragged on for George. He only hoped that it was not doing so for the students. At last the class ended, and he dismissed everyone and hurried out into the hall. He rushed to his office and deposited his books and papers on his desk, then went out looking for the two lawmen. He found them just coming out of the principal's office.

"Rider," he called. "Elwood."

" '*Siyo*, George," said Rider.

"George?" said Lovely. "This here can't be old George Tanner. He looks like some eastern dude to me."

"Knock it off, Elwood," said George. "Come on down to my office. I've got something to tell you."

"Ain't you supposed to be teaching?" asked Rider.

"I've got a few minutes," said George. "Come on."

He led the way to his office, and when all three men were inside, he shut the door behind them. He pulled two chairs up close to the desk for Rider and Lovely to sit on. Then he went around and sat on the other side. He picked up Chris Lang's journal and held it out for them to see.

"I read this last night," he said.

"What is it?" asked Lovely.

"It's a journal that Chris kept," said George. "He wrote something in it just about every day, starting with the day Councilman Peck hired him for this job. Lee and Exie found it the day they went through Chris's things. It wasn't here. He had it at home."

George thumbed through the pages, working his way toward the final entries.

"If he didn't write down in there who it was that killed him," said Lovely, "I don't see what good it's going to do us."

"Listen to this," said George. " 'I find myself in a quandary here. I am still new on my job, and it is a very awkward thing for the recent addition to start to stir up trouble. Yet I have become aware of something that needs to be told. At the very least it needs to be thoroughly investigated to determine whether or not my strong suspicions are valid. I hope they are not, but if they are, they must be confirmed, and soon.' "

George stopped reading and turned a page. Rider rubbed his chin and waited for more.

"What's he talking about?" said Lovely.

"Here," said George, turning to a new page.

" 'I am the more convinced about the rightness of my suspicions concerning a certain colleague of mine, but the charges, if leveled, by me or by anyone else, are so horrible that without absolute proof, I will not even commit them to writing in this private format, nor dare to record the name of the suspected scoundrel.' "

"Damn," said Lovely. "That there's our killer, ain't it?"

"Is there any more, George?" Rider asked.

"Just this," said George. He flipped two pages, then read again. " 'I think he knows that I am onto him.' That's all." He put the book down on the desktop and reached for the notepad. "That's all the relevant journal entries anyhow. But there is this. It's a pad that Lee found right here on this desk. There's only one note: 'Kenyon College.' "

"That's all?" asked Lovely.

"Yes," said George, "except that Lee asked Mr. Downing if this note meant anything to him. She told him where she found it, and Downing recalled that Chris had asked him where Carl Morrison had been before coming here, and Downing told him."

"Kenyon College?" said Rider.

"Kenyon College," said George.

"So it's a good guess that this Morrison is the fellow Lang was writing about in that journal," said Lovely. "He said there'd ought to be an investigation, and then he went and asked about Morrison."

"It stands to reason," said George.

"Let's go get the bastard," said Lovely.

"Hold your horses, Elwood," said Rider. "We got no proof. Let's try to ease up on him. Let's just go on with what we were doing, talking to everyone out here, and when it comes his turn, we'll talk to him. But we won't talk to him no different than anyone else. Not yet. If he is the killer, we don't want to spook him. Not till we've got something on him that we can hold him with."

"Hell," said Lovely, "we know he was here."

"What's that?" said George.

"That's right," said Rider. "Mr. Downing told us that Morrison was on duty the night of the killing, with the boys upstairs, the ones who live here. Most go home on weekends, he said, but there's always a few who stay. Someone has to stay with them, and that night it was Morrison."

"If any mail has come in for Chris since — since he was killed," said George, "what would become of it?"

"I expect the postmaster'd be holding it," said Rider.

"Can you get it?"

"I can," said Lovely, "if it's U.S. mail. What're we looking for?"

"A letter from Kenyon College," said George. "I can't think of any reason for

Chris to want to know where Morrison had come from, unless it was to write to them and ask about him."

"He might not have got around to it," said Lovely, "but I'll check on it and see."

"And there's another thing," said George. "Rider, I think you ought to do this yourself."

"What is it, George?"

"Talk to Tommy Snail. He was sick in bed upstairs here, and he told Mr. Downing that he was going home. He said nothing would make him go up there again, and he was ready to walk all the way out to his home in Lost City if he had to. Mr. Downing drove him home."

George pulled a watch out of his pocket and gave it a quick look.

"I have to get to class," he said. "Feel free to use my office while you're here. I'll see you later."

George grabbed a couple of books and hurried out the door. Lovely flopped back in his chair.

"Damn, Rider," he said, "I believe George has come up with something there."

"I figured he would," said Rider.

"Hell, you never meant to give up old George, did you. You're just using him as a plant, a kind of a spy."

"No," said Rider. "I mean for George to stay on here, if he takes to it, and so far it looks like he is. But if he can help us out on this at the same time, well, ain't nothing wrong with that, is there?"

"Not a damn thing," said Lovely, standing up and stretching. "Well, what do we do now?"

"Why don't we put off the rest of these interviews," suggested Rider, "and go out and take George's advice."

Carl Morrison stood beside an upstairs window and watched as Rider and Lovely mounted their horses in front of the building. He watched them turn the horses and ride away. He knew they had been interviewing the staff and faculty of the seminary, and he wondered why they were leaving so early. He wondered why they had not got around to him. He noticed that when the two riders reached the end of the lane which led up to the front door, they turned and rode in opposite directions. He hurried down the stairs and went straight to the principal's office.

"Mr. Downing," he said, barging in, "have those lawmen concluded their investigation?"

Downing looked up, surprised by Morrison's sudden intrusion.

"Why, no," he said. "I think they've only just begun."

"They just left. Both of them."

"That's strange," said Downing. "Well, they'll probably be back."

"Yes," said Morrison. "I'm sure they will."

Lovely went through the stack of mail the postmaster had put on the counter in front of him, examining each piece carefully for some indication of where it had come from. Suddenly he lifted one up and held it in front of his eyes.

"Hot damn," he said. "Hot damn."

He had to fill out a form for the postmaster in order to take the letter away, but it was a short form, and he didn't mind at all. He understood well the necessity of bureaucratic paperwork.

"We work for the same boss," he said as he handed the completed form to the postmaster.

It was past noon by the time Go-Ahead Rider found the home of Tommy Snail in Lost City. There was no city there, not even a small village. Rather, Lost City was a community of homes scattered through the wooded hills, the residents of which tended to gather together for church and for special occasions. When Rider rode up toward the house, Ben Snail came out the front door.

"Go-Ahead?" he said, speaking in Cherokee. "That you?"

" 'Siyo, Ben," said Rider. "Are you well?"

"Pretty good," said Snail. "What brings you all the way out here?"

"I came to have a talk with your son, Tommy. Is he at home?"

"He's in the house, in bed," said Snail. "He's sick. He came home from school. His mother went to get old Selly to bring her here to doctor him. Is Tommy in some kind of trouble?"

"No, he's not in trouble, but he might be able to help me out with some information. Can I talk to him?"

"I guess so," said Snail. "Come on in."

Snail led the way into the house, a small log cabin, and Rider followed. It was dark inside, but a blaze glowed in the fireplace, casting eerie glimmers and shadows throughout the warm room. Rider pulled off his big coat and his hat and glanced around.

"Just put them down anywhere," said Snail.

Rider dropped them on a nearby chair. He had already spotted Tommy on a bed against the back wall. He glanced at Snail, and Snail gestured toward the bed.

"Go on," he said. "Tommy. Go-Ahead Rider is here to talk to you. The sheriff. Are you awake?"

"Yes," said Tommy, his voice weak.

Rider pulled a chair up close to the edge of Tommy's bed. The boy looked afraid. He also looked sick. He was sweating.

"Tommy," said Rider, continuing to use the Cherokee language, "don't be afraid of me. I'm not here to arrest you. I just want to ask you some questions. Okay?"

"Okay," said Tommy.

"I want you to know that Coley Fletcher came to town with his father. They paid the hotel for the room and for the damages, and they paid for the horses. Coley even went to Mr. Downing at the school and told him everything. They let him resign from the school, and he's gone home with his father."

"He's not in jail?" said Tommy.

"No."

"I'm glad."

"Tommy, why did you spend the weekend running around with Coley?" Rider asked. "They told me at the school that you usually come home on weekends. When you don't come home, you stay at the school. Why'd you go out with Coley like that?"

Tommy lowered his eyelids.

"I don't know," he said. "He asked me."

"That's all?"

Tommy made no response.

"When you were sick in bed at school," said Rider, "you told Mr. Downing that you were coming home. You said that you wouldn't go back upstairs. Why was that, Tommy?"

"I just wanted to come home," said Tommy. "I was homesick."

"That's all?"

"I feel better at home. I'll get well faster."

"I do too," said Rider, "but you had been staying at the school for some time. You must have gotten used to it. Mr. Downing said that you were doing real well. All of a sudden, you didn't stay at school on the weekend, and then you wouldn't stay in bed, even though you were sick. Mr. Downing told me that you threatened to walk all the way home. You're sick, and it's cold outside. Tell me about it, Tommy."

"Tommy," said Ben Snail, "if there's something you're not telling Go-Ahead, I think you'd better tell it."

Rider stood up and stepped over close to Snail.

"Ben," he said in a low voice, "would you wait outside?"

Snail wrapped a blanket around his shoulders and went out into the yard. Rider went back to the chair by the bed.

"What is it, Tommy?" he said.

Tommy turned his head away.

"Listen to me," said Rider. "Somebody murdered Mr. Lang. You liked Mr. Lang, didn't you?"

"Yes."

"Then help me, Tommy. We believe that someone at the school killed Mr. Lang. He found out something about someone, and he was checking up on that person. We think maybe that person killed him. Do you know anything that might help us?"

"He put his hands on me," said Tommy.

"Who?"

"Mr. Morrison. He came up while I was

asleep in bed. He reached under the sheets, and he put his hands on — He put his hands on me."

"When did this happen?"

"It was Thursday night. Then on Friday, Coley asked me to spend the weekend with him in Tahlequah. He said he'd get us a room in the hotel. I didn't have any money, or I would have taken the train home for the weekend. I didn't want to stay at school — Mr. Morrison had the duty."

"Is that also why you got out of your sickbed to come home?" Rider asked.

Tommy nodded his head slowly.

"Yes," he said.

"Tommy," said Rider, "you rest up and get well. Try not to worry about any of this. When you get better, you go on back to school. Mr. Morrison won't be there any-more. I promise you."

—23—

When George finished with his last class, he rushed out to his buggy and drove straight to the National Prison. He left the buggy standing in the street and ran into the office. He found Delbert Swim sitting at the small desk and Elwood Lovely pacing the floor. Lovely turned quickly when George came bursting in.

"Oh," he said, "it's you."

"Sorry to disappoint you," said George. "Where's Rider?"

"That's why I'm disappointed," said Lovely. "I was looking for Rider when you came in. He went out to talk to Tommy Snail."

"Did you find anything?" George asked.

"Just look at this," said Lovely, taking two long strides over to Rider's desk and slapping a piece of paper down on the desktop. George hurried over to stand beside him, and both men leaned over the paper to read.

"It's from Kenyon College," said George.

"You sure had that one figured right," said Lovely. "Go on. Read it."

My dear Mr. Lang,
Regarding your recent inquiry, Mr. Carl

Morrison was indeed a member of our faculty up until last May. I wrote him a letter of recommendation to the principal of your school with the following understanding: that he submit to me a letter of resignation, and that he assure me that he would work very hard at mending his ways. He did not hesitate to give me such assurances. Indeed, he wept so bitterly in my office that I was firmly convinced that he had repented of his sins. Even so, the letter I furnished him was hardly glowing.

I had hoped that I would never have occasion to make mention of the reasons for Mr. Morrison's departure from Kenyon College, and I tremble at writing the words even now. But obviously he has not mended his ways, and so I am compelled to proceed.

Mr. Morrison was asked to resign from Kenyon College because of our clear perception that he was taking, shall I say, an unhealthy interest in the younger boys. I don't know how to put it any more delicately.

I can only close this missive by offering the following advice: Do not be lenient, as I was. Do not be taken in by a show of contrition. He has had his second chance. Do not give him a third.

Very humbly yours,

Charles O. Stevenson, Dean

"Well, what do you say?" said Lovely. "Is that a motive for murder?"

"It's disgusting," said Swim. "That's what it is."

"It would seem to be," said George. "It's certainly what Chris was writing about in his journal, and Morrison is the man Chris was investigating. There's no question about that."

"And," said Lovely, "Lang wrote in that book that the man was onto him."

"Yes, and at the very least, discovery would mean that he would lose his job, and I don't think that Mr. Downing would have let him off as easy as this Stevenson did. He might kill to keep his secret."

"He was in the building," said Lovely. "I think we've got a case."

"I think he's the one, all right," said George, "but a trial could go either way. Why don't you wait and see what Rider thinks?"

"Yeah," said Lovely. "That's what I was going to do anyhow."

"I think I'll get on home now," said George. "Delbert, are you carrying my Starr revolver?"

"Huh? Oh, no. I've got a Colt here."

"Where's the Starr, then?"

"I think it's in Rider's desk."

George went around behind the big desk and opened a drawer. The Starr was there in its holster. George pulled it out and wrapped the belt around his waist. He glanced up and saw Lovely and Swim watching him with curiosity.

"I've missed it," he said with a casual shrug. "That's all. I've worn it so long that I don't feel right without it. And I am still a deputy sheriff. I didn't quit, remember? I'm just on leave."

He fastened the buckle, gave the rig a hitch, then walked to the door.

"I'll see you boys later," he said, and he walked out the door. A moment later, Swim and Lovely could hear the sounds of his buggy rolling down the street.

But George did not drive home. Instead he drove his buggy back to the seminary and parked it beside the front door. He got out of the buggy and tried the door. It was locked. He took his key out of his pocket and let himself in, but he did not bother locking the door again behind himself. He walked down the hallway past his office and onto the stairs that would lead him up to the second floor, the dormitory where the boys who were residents had their beds.

When Rider returned to his office, he found Swim and Lovely waiting for him. Lovely showed him the letter from the dean at Kenyon College and summarized the conversation with George.

"Well, it all fits," said Rider. "That's exactly

why Tommy Snail wanted to get away from the school. Somehow or other, old Chris Lang found out about Morrison, or at least suspected him pretty strongly. He started his own private investigation, but Morrison learned about it."

"And killed Lang," added Lovely.

"It looks that way to me," said Rider.

"You think we got enough on him?" asked Lovely.

"It's all circumstantial," said Rider, "but I bet a jury would convict him. For sure it's enough to bring him in for questioning."

"Let's go get the son of a bitch," said Lovely.

"You want me to go along?" asked Swim.

"No, Delbert," said Rider, "I'd rather you stay here and keep an eye on things till we get back. The two of us can handle Morrison all right."

George stopped at the top of the stairs. He had not been on the second floor before. He was looking down a long hallway which ran down the middle of the floor. Doors leading to rooms were on both sides of the hall. He opened the first door on his right and looked in. It appeared to be an office, but no one was there. He closed it and tried the door on his left. That room contained a bureau and a bed. Again, no one was in the room.

George started walking down the hall, and then he heard voices. He moved toward them. They got louder. He tried a door, and it opened into a large dormitory with two rows of beds. Half a dozen boys were in the big room.

It was still early evening, and the boys were dressed and lounging about. A couple of them were actually reading. One, whom George recognized from one of his classes, was reading Plutarch. The others, divided into three small groups, were talking casually. When George stepped into the room, they all looked at him, and the talking ceased.

"Mr. Tanner," said one of the boys. "What are you doing here?"

"Just looking around," said George. He noticed that the boys were staring at the gun on his hip. "Who's on duty tonight?"

"I don't know," said the boy.

"Mr. Jones was supposed to be," said another boy, "but I think Mr. Morrison traded with him."

"Is Morrison here then?" asked George.

"I haven't seen him."

"Where does he stay when he's on duty?"

"He has a room across the hall," said the boy with the open Plutarch. "He might be over there."

George moved to the center of the room and gestured for the boys to gather around him.

"Come here," he said. "Come over here for a minute. I want to talk to all of you."

The boys moved in close around him.

"What?"

"What is it?"

"What do you want?"

"How do you boys feel about Mr. Morrison?" George asked them, and suddenly they were all quiet. "Well, come on. Do you like him?"

"No," said the Plutarch scholar.

"Why not?"

Again there was silence.

"What about the rest of you? Do you like him?"

"He's funny," said another boy.

"Funny?" said George. "How do you mean?"

"You know. Funny."

"He tells jokes?"

"No. Not like that. He looks at you funny, and he's always putting his hands on you. And he tries to get you off by yourself all the time."

"He got me in his room one time," said Plutarch. "He talked real weird, and he showed me a knife. I ran out of there as fast as I could. He saw me later in the hallway, and he whispered that I better keep my mouth shut if I knew what was good for me."

"This knife," said George. "What did it look like?"

"I don't know. A knife. A real big one. About this long."

259

"Would you recognize it if you saw it again?"

"I don't know. Maybe. I think I would."

"Okay, boys," said George. "I want you all to stay here. Is Mr. Morrison's room the one straight across the hall from here?"

"Yeah. Right there," said a boy, pointing. "What are you going to do?"

"I'm just going to see if he's over there. You all stay put now."

George moved to the door, and he heard the voices whispering behind him.

"He's going to shoot old Morrison."

"No he's not."

"Sure he is. You see that gun?"

"I hope he does. I hope he kills him."

George stepped across the hall and opened the door. Again he found an empty room. There was a rumpled bed, and there was a desk with a couple of books on top of it. There was also a leather sheath for a large knife, and it was empty. It was the right size. George felt the hairs on the back of his neck stand up. He whirled around, but no one was behind him. No one else was in the room.

He stepped out into the hallway again, and then he walked its length, opening each door and checking each room. Still he did not find Morrison. He found no one. There was no one on the second floor, it seemed, but himself and the boys in the dormitory room. He walked back to the head of the stairway. If

Morrison is in the building, he thought, he must be downstairs.

Suddenly he was hit hard from behind, as if an ancient Greek wrestler had run into him, and he went flying out over the stairs. He yelled out loud as he fell, and he tried to duck his head in preparation for the landing. He hit the stairs hard, and he rolled, then turned sideways and tumbled. About halfway down, he thought that he had regained control of his body. His feet were toward the bottom of the stairs, and he tried to stand up. At the same time, he pulled the Starr revolver from his holster and whipped it up toward the mysterious figure that loomed over him at the top of the stairs.

But the momentum was too much for him. He fell backward, and as he did, he dropped the revolver. He rolled end over end the rest of the way down and wound up sprawled on the floor at the bottom of the stairs.

He felt like every muscle had been bruised, every bone bumped. With a groan he raised his head, and he saw that the figure that had been at the top of the stairs was now standing just over him, and was raising a long pole as if to strike. He recognized the weapon as one of the poles designed to open and close a transom over a door, and he recognized the figure as Morrison.

With a tremendous effort, George rolled to his right, just in time to avoid the blow.

261

Morrison raised the pole again. Again he swung it, and again George rolled out from under it just in time. He raised himself up almost to a sitting position and scooted backward until he had pressed himself against an office door. There was no place else to go, and Morrison had drawn the pole back as if to hurl it like a spear. George braced himself for the terrible blow, and then flinched at the unexpected sound of an explosion.

Morrison stood for a moment like a statue of a spear-thrower poised for the toss. His mouth was open, and his face was contorted with what might have been agony or hatred or desperation. A splotch of dark red had appeared on his shirtfront. Slowly his fingers relaxed, and the pole fell from his grasp and clattered on the floor. A moment later, Morrison, dead on his feet, fell forward, stiff as a board.

Gasping for breath and amazed to be alive, George looked down the hallway to see Rider, a big Colt in his right hand, and Elwood Lovely, standing wide-eyed beside him.

"George," said Rider. "You all right?"

"Yeah, I think so," said George. "Thanks to you. I'm bruised all over, but I don't think anything's broken."

Lovely knelt beside the body and gave it a quick examination. Then he looked over at George.

"Morrison?" he said.

"Morrison," said George. With a painful groan, he tried to get himself to his feet.

"Hold on there, George," said Rider. "Take it easy."

"Rider, there's a bunch of boys up there, probably scared to death. I've got to go tell them that everything's all right here."

"You settle back and take it easy," said Rider. "I'll go tell them."

He started up the stairs, but Elwood Lovely stopped him.

"Rider."

Rider paused and looked over his shoulder. "Yeah?"

"Rider, this here's a white man. This Morrison. Right?"

"That's right," said Rider. "He sure ain't one of ours."

"Well then," said Lovely, "I guess it was my shot that killed him. Not yours."

"I guess," said Rider, and he continued his way up the stairs. Lovely looked over at George.

"It'll look better on the report that way," he said.

"I saw the whole thing," said George. "It was your shot."

—24—

The next day, Elwood Lovely took his lone prisoner, Forbes Winters, and a whole stack of paperwork with him back to Muskogee. George paid Rider a visit after his school day was done, and they discussed the details of the murder case. There were some things that had never quite fit together, things such as the missing keys and the lamp that had been put out. They could only assume that Morrison had taken the keys to throw suspicion on someone from outside, and had put out the light to keep anyone else from checking in on Lang quite as soon as they might have had the lamp stayed on.

Neither man admitted it out loud to the other, but they both knew that they really had no more proof of the guilt of Morrison than they had of, say, Peck. According to the physical evidence, it was still quite possible that Peck could have been the guilty party. But Peck's attitude had convinced George that he was not the one.

The strongest evidence against Morrison was, of course, the fact that he had attacked George, and that in itself did not prove that he had killed Lang. But the circumstantial evidence was powerful, and it was enough to satisfy George, Rider, and Elwood Lovely, who had written it all up in his report, which also said that Lovely had killed Morrison in the line of duty.

Go-Ahead Rider was not bothered at all by that false information in the federal report. He did not want to be bothered by any federal inquiries, and he had never been one to carve notches on the handles of his Colts.

Rider talked to Judge Boley about Willit Barnes, and the judge assured Rider that he would do everything he could to keep the trial in the Cherokee courts. True, Shadrach Barnes had been a white man, but he had married a Cherokee woman in order to obtain citizenship rights in the Cherokee Nation. Boley thought that he would have no trouble keeping the trial at home. He also opined that the court might give some consideration to the fact of Shadrach's terrible abuse of his son when the time for sentencing came around.

Winters, it seemed, would probably go to jail for a long time, for by the time Lovely finally got him to a federal jail, he had charged the railroad man not only with possessing liquor in the Cherokee Nation, but also with breaking jail, resisting arrest, assaulting an officer of the law, and being an accessory to two murders. There was no reason to assume that the charges would not stick.

Winters's sometime partner, Ira Peck, did indeed turn in his letter of resignation from the Cherokee National Council, but he did not return to his Sequoyah District home. He remained in his Tahlequah home, a safe distance from the voters who had elected him, and he did not often leave his house.

Coley Fletcher had gone home with his father to concentrate on becoming the best rancher he could be. No charges were filed against Fletcher by either the Cherokee Nation or the federal government.

In the beginning, Go-Ahead Rider wondered how much time it would take for Delbert Swim to become half as good a deputy as George Tanner had been, but he soon realized that there would never be enough time. He resigned himself to having to be content with less, for with each passing day it was more obvious that George was more than content with his new profession.

Tommy Snail returned to school, where Mr. Tanner soon became his favorite teacher.